Newton & Einstein, Stuff T

Prologue

Long before Isaac Newton or Albert Einstein was born, the ancient Greeks devoted great effort to pondering the world and the meaning of their lives in it. The Greeks were keen observers of nature and the human condition. What they observed led them to conclude that supernatural beings living on a mythical Mount Olympus influenced their daily lives, to advantage for some people and disadvantage for others. If a battle went well for you then the Gods on Mount Olympus favored you that day. If the battle didn't go well, it was obvious you had offended the Gods and paid the price accordingly. The accepted belief was that these Gods entertained themselves by playing games with peoples' successes or failures, suffering or affluence, often in trivial ways other than on the battlefield. Some Gods were benevolent, while others were cruel and vengeful. The Greeks regarded them that way based on sound evidence.

While we (most of us, anyway) don't believe in Zeus, Athena, Poseidon, Apollo, etc. in modern times, the observations that lead the Greeks to believe in mythical Gods with benevolent/malevolent intentions cannot be dismissed. Clearly they were onto something! Such observations have continued to accumulate for past millennia up to the present day with no consistent explanation. They point inevitably to the supposition that there is an unseen 'presence' that influences our daily lives in ways we can observe, but can't explain using the laws of physics and probability, as we understand them. But before you jump to the conclusion that I am referring to a "deity", "higher being" or "creator" in a religious context, let me assure you I am not! The 'presence' I am referring to has never created anything except chaos.

Before we can examine this 'presence' we must perform an essential (but not very important) task of giving it a name. I could, of course, call it Zeus or Athena, but those names have been repeatedly discredited, and besides that would be plagiarizing the splendid achievements of the Greeks. I chose instead to recall a TV ad (for margarine) from the 1970's that ended with the catch phrase, "It's not nice to fool with Mother Nature!" The meaning was quite clear

Newton & Einstein, Stuff They Didn't Tell You

– if you get on the wrong side of Mother Nature, she will take her revenge in more sinister and devious ways than you can possibly imagine! In that context it seems appropriate to borrow such a characterization for this discussion, as you will see.

By the way, such ads in the 1970's were not intended to denigrate either motherhood or nature, and in those days virtually no one would have been offended by such a phrase. But it's the 21st Century, so as a general disclaimer I must state that I mean no disrespect in using the term "Mother Nature" throughout this book. If the reader finds the term offensive I would suggest substituting any other term (including abject profanity) of your choice. I won't be offended at all.

Newton & Einstein, Stuff They Didn't Tell You

Introduction

Like most engineering students in the late 1960's I took all the required courses in applied and theoretical physics. I accepted Isaac Newton's physical laws and Albert Einstein's theories as a (mostly) rational explanation of how the universe works. In fact, I relied on these laws and theories for a successful thirty-six year career in the chemical and nuclear industries. However, over the years it has become increasingly obvious to me that there are some additional laws of physics and probability, which neither Newton nor Einstein told us about. Either they observed these phenomena but chose not to point them out to the rest of us, or these learned gentlemen failed to observe them at all (for reasons I shall explain in this book). In any case, it is my intent to expose these phenomena and their consequences (real and imagined) once and for all herein.

If you read further you may find yourself nodding and smiling because those weird things that keep happening to you will begin to make sense, now that you understand the unseen forces behind them. On the other hand, you may conclude the world this book describes is obviously absurd and implausible.

This book is intended to provide hope for those who live in that implausible world, and the realization that they are not alone.

Newton & Einstein, Stuff They Didn't Tell You

TABLE OF CONTENTS

Prologue 1
Introduction 3
Chapter One - What Makes Things Work, or NOT! 6
Chapter Two - So What Type Are You? 9
Chapter Three - The Nature of Mother Nature 20
Chapter Four - Special Physical Laws I 25
Chapter Five - Special Physical Laws II 42
Chapter Six - Mind Games I 57
Chapter Seven - Mind Games II 69
Chapter Eight - Mind Games III 80
Chapter Nine - Maintaining Your Sanity 92
Chapter Ten - Great Expectations (NOT) 102
Chapter Eleven - Computing Your Odds 111
Chapter Twelve - Games of Chance 121
Chapter Fourteen - Packaging your Frustration 127
Chapter Fifteen - Timing is Everything 135
Chapter Sixteen - So What is Time? 142
Chapter Seventeen - Getting From A to B 154
Chapter Eighteen - Paths You Did Not Choose 162
Chapter Nineteen - Age Matters 170
Chapter Twenty - Constructing a Win-Win 181
Chapter Twenty-One - Leveling the Playing Field 190
Chapter Twenty-Two - Can We? – Should We? 198
Chapter Twenty-Three - Conclusions (in Your Head) 204
Chapter Twenty-Four - One last point! 206
Related Essays 207

Newton & Einstein, Stuff They Didn't Tell You

Chapter One
What Makes Things Work, or NOT!

God does not play dice with the universe – Albert Einstein

God doesn't roll dice to determine how the universe works. I agree with him on that point. It's obvious he delegated that function instead to Mother Nature. Some of us find Mother Nature plays dice with our lives every day; only the dice are loaded.

This book is about the ways in which Mother Nature affects the daily lives of millions of people, and the special laws of physics and probability she uses to make those of her choosing miserable.

In the engineering profession we sometimes say that "Mother Nature sides with the hidden flaw" – meaning that things you design and build will not work the way you want them to, but you won't discover the difficulty until late in the project when it's very embarrassing and expensive to fix.

It's been claimed, "Mother Nature is a bitch!" If that means she'll screw you anytime in any way she can, then I'm forced to agree.

For some of us Mother Nature can be really mean spirited. Shortly after my retirement I decided to relocate to another state to improve my chances of getting some part time consulting work. This meant getting a driver's license in my new state of residence. As I approached the service counter I was informed that the computers were down and no applications for driver's licenses could be processed until they came back up. I asked, "When will the computers be back up?" No one seemed to know. As I looked around the room at the crowd that was waiting, it occurred to me that most of these people had taken time off from their jobs, perhaps with loss of pay, just to sit and wait for a computer to start working again. Add to that the six idle people who were being paid to process our driver's license requests.

Mother Nature had us all right were she wanted us. If frustration cost ten cents

Newton & Einstein, Stuff They Didn't Tell You

per pound, that room was worth at least $1 million. After about two hours we were informed that the computers were back up, at least temporarily, and we could now begin waiting until our number was called. Fortunately, all the computers in the world haven't yet become "self-aware" and taken over everything as portrayed in the "Terminator" movies. If (when) that happens I suppose none of us will be allowed to drive a car anymore.

Mother Nature has the edge.

Since it is clearly impossible for us to think of everything that can go wrong, there are always "opportunities" for Mother Nature to foul things up. Yes, we have made it harder for her since we invented high-speed computers, fault trees, and all sorts of other technology to help us identify failures before they happen. But to her credit, Mother Nature has taken advantage of these technologies to generate new and more expensive ways to make things not work.

A good example is your family car. Once upon a time you could take your family car to the local mechanic who would simply figure out what was wrong and fix it. Not any more! If you bought your car in the last decade you know that everything is now run by one of several onboard computers. When your car doesn't run properly, you take it back to the dealership (local mechanics can't help you) and they start replacing computer boards until they find one that makes the car run properly again.

The good news for them is they don't get their hands dirty messing around with your engine and stuff. The double bad news for you is that the new onboard computers have many more failure modes (including ones nobody has thought of yet) than your old car had. Plus new computer boards cost many times more than the automobile parts your local mechanic used to bill you for.

And don't try to get the service department to explain what was wrong with your car because they don't have a clue. All they can say is that it's fixed and you need to pay the lady at the counter up front. We'll talk more about computers and all things electronic in a later chapter. You'll see why Mother Nature loves electronic stuff.

Newton & Einstein, Stuff They Didn't Tell You

Mother Nature has another advantage. She knows what you want, especially when you are under stress. Ever have one of those days when nothing seems to go right? The harder you try to get something done, the more resistance you encounter. It's like that Star Trek episode where the Enterprise was caught in an energy field. The energy field draws its strength from the ship's engines so it grows ever stronger the more the ship tries to escape.

And the clever part is that the resistance to whatever you are trying to accomplish is always within the realm of random chance. It's like flipping a coin ten times and getting heads every time - unlikely, but not impossible. So you can't quite convince yourself that the dead battery on your cell phone, plus the wreck on the highway, plus Jenny getting sick at school that morning, plus your coworker's coffee on your new suit, all before lunch, really represents the involvement of a sinister force in the universe. Actually it's just Mother Nature reading your mind and having some fun at your expense.

I'll say a lot more about Mother Nature and your relationship with her (whether you want one or not) in later chapters.

But before you ask, I can't tell you where Mother Nature came from. All I know is she's always been there for me. Now, for those of you who say I am making this stuff up, it's time to talk about the types of people in the universe, or at least the ones on Earth.

Newton & Einstein, Stuff They Didn't Tell You

**Chapter Two
So What Type Are You?**

I do not know what I may appear to the world, but to myself I seem to have been only like a boy playing on the seashore, and diverting myself in now and then finding a smoother pebble or a prettier shell than ordinary, whilst the great ocean of truth lay all undiscovered before me - Isaac Newton

If you're thinking this is just another scheme to categorize people for some narrow self-serving purpose, you're right.

But I've made it easy. Rather than wading through some list of character traits that don't seem to apply to any real person you know, I'm giving you only two choices. To make it even easier, one of those choices is so obvious you probably already know that you're it. So, let's talk about all those other more fortunate people.

There are those who are blessed from birth with Mother Nature's ambivalence. She either counts you as one of her very rare favorites, or else she couldn't care less. Either way you can start each and every day with confidence that you have at least an even chance. For simplicity we can refer to these people as Type Y (Y for yes). Type Y people are optimistic and extremely logical. Why shouldn't they be – life has been fair to them. A good example of a Type Y is Mr. Spock on the television series Star Trek. You may recall that Mr. Spock firmly believed there was a logical explanation for everything.

Type Y's tend to have a positive attitude, are confident in their ability to succeed, and like to point out the substantial obstacles they have overcome in life.

A common characteristic of these folks is the shared belief that random chance controls much of what goes on in the world. That's because in their world it does! Type Y's ignore Mother Nature because she ignores them. They are

Newton & Einstein, Stuff They Didn't Tell You

seldom affected by the special physical laws described in this book, and usually fail to notice that they exist at all. In general, Y's tend to lead dull lives with things going their way at least half the time. Newton and Einstein may have been Type Y's and, as a result, failed to notice the special physical laws I'm about to describe.

Then there are the other folks who we shall call Type N (N for no).

These folks are seasoned by hard experience. That experience comes from having lived in a world where Mother Nature controls the odds, a world that is quite different from that of the Type Y's. Type N's are often pessimistic. Why shouldn't they be – Mother Nature has screwed them whenever she could get away with it. Type N's sometimes have negative attitudes born of sad memories of futility. They are often cynical and superstitious (they call it being realistic), cautious when making promises and suspicious of those who make promises to them.

Type N people are accustomed to disappointment, but refuse to be crushed by it. They discover at an early age that they have to work three times as hard as everyone else to make something good happen. Mother Nature uses the principle of Maximum Effort (described in Chapter Five) to make it so. Type N's are very good at alternative planning. They are accustomed to considering multiple failures up to the limits that random chance will permit, identifying multiple ways around those failures. It's sort of like running in a track meet. If you are a Type Y, the hurtles are placed at standard intervals and you get to see them before the race starts; if you are Type N you don't know where or how many hurtles there will be until they pop up at random during the race.

Clearly Type N people have to be the more versatile and agile thinkers!

Here are just of few of the tell-tale signs that you are a Type N:
- Four out of five green traffic signals turn yellow just before you get to them. This not only makes you stop but also guarantees the maximum wait time before the next green light.

Newton & Einstein, Stuff They Didn't Tell You

- A store has the item you have been looking for and in every size (or color, etc.) except the one you need.
- You park and enter the shopping mall to find that the store you want is at the other end of the mall.
- You get into the shortest line at the bank, and then the person in front of you demands a complete printout of their last three months transactions, followed by a detailed explanation as to why their account is overdrawn.
- The ATM at your bank is being serviced by Wells Fargo when you want to withdraw some cash, on three separate occasions in the same week.
- It's a Monday holiday in July and the propane tank on your gas grill goes empty when you are half way through cooking steaks for your boss and his wife, who flew down from Pittsburg just to have one of your famous rib-eyes.
- You agree to use a random number system to determine who will drive each day in your five-person carpool, and your number comes up six times in the first two weeks.
- You have only five items so you go to the express checkout lane in the grocery store; only the person in front of you wants to buy an item with no bar code. You are forced to witness the store manager and assistant manager getting into a heated argument for 20 minutes trying to determine the correct price.
- The toilet paper dispenser jams in the public restroom, not only in your stall but in the other three stalls as well.
- You usually fail to notice that the address doesn't show in the little plastic window or that you left the check out until after you seal the envelope.
- Any action that normally takes only one hand will suddenly take both hands, if one hand is holding something you don't want to let go of.
- Some drug dealer has scratched his cell phone number into the paint on the restroom wall, and you notice it's your daughter's cell phone number except for the area code.

One famous Type N was the inept French police lieutenant played by Peter

Newton & Einstein, Stuff They Didn't Tell You

Sellers in the Pink Panther movies. I remember sitting in the theatre and noticing people's reactions to the antics occurring on the screen. Some were clearly convinced that whoever wrote the script had gone beyond the ridiculous. Others were smiling because they recognized an unmistakable similarity to what they themselves go through every day.

Television writers gave us an equally famous Type N when they created the character of Al Bundy in the series "Married with Children". Most of the Type Y's I know proudly proclaimed Al Bundy's character as stupidly pathetic and totally unrealistic. These folks never found "Married with Children" worth watching. Conversely, if you know any Type N's you won't be surprised to discover that they were avid fans of the series and tried to catch the reruns when they were on. Why? Because it's comforting to observe someone (even if fictional) who Mother Nature has abused more than the person they see in the mirror every morning. Al Bundy was the "poster child" for all us Type N's!

If you are thinking that Type N's must be a small minority of the Earth's population, consider the wide popularity of the (fictional) characters just mentioned.

When P. T. Barnum said, "There's a sucker born every minute" he was talking about us N's. Is being a Type N hereditary? My father was one. He had great mechanical aptitude, but struggled with things electronic. Maybe that's because when he was born electronics still meant radios made with vacuum tubes and the words "television" and "computer" didn't exist. Regardless, simple devices like the TV remote control or the cable box were sources of endless frustration for my Dad. It has to do with the way the cable box is programmed. While you are watching one channel you can push a button to see the menu of programs available on other channels. Push the button again and you're back on the channel you were watching, or maybe you're not.

And if you push the menu button again the screen may show the menu starting with the channel you were watching, or it may start instead with Channel 1. Neither of us were ever able to "break the code" that apparently decides whether the menu starts with Channel 1 or some other channel, perhaps the one you were

Newton & Einstein, Stuff They Didn't Tell You

watching. Is Mother Nature somehow involved in all of this? I'm betting she is, even though I can't prove it.

My daughter and both my sons are Type Y's. They must have gotten it from their mother. They certainly didn't get it from me. It's such a joy to see how smoothly their lives run. And even when it doesn't, I still marvel at how things come out. For example, my oldest son who is in the United States Air Force was diagnosed one summer with Aplastic Anemia. This is a condition where your bone marrow stops producing blood cells and you need frequent blood transfusions to stay alive. The cure is to get a bone marrow transplant from someone who has healthy bone marrow. But there's a catch. The bone marrow donor needs to be a close match, usually meaning a blood relative like a brother or sister.

Here are the facts:
- First, my son happens to have both a brother and a sister,
- Second, both his brother and sister turned out to be exact matches for the bone marrow transplant (there was only one chance in three that either of them would be a match),
- Third, both his brother and sister also happen to be his same blood type (further simplifying the transplant procedure),
- Fourth, his brother is about 6' 4" tall and could easily donate the one and a half liters of bone marrow needed without serious or lasting affect,
- Fifth, he got through the chemotherapy prior the transplant without serious complications,
- Sixth, his body accepted the transplant with only minor "Graft vs. Host Disease" complications,
- Seventh, the United States Air Force housed him and his wife near the hospital for the duration of his treatment (approximately 5 months),
- Eighth, all medical expenses totaling over $400,000 were paid by the Air Force,
- Ninth, the Air Force returned him to active duty status,
- Tenth, one year later he had fully recovered from a disease considered relatively incurable a few decades ago.

Newton & Einstein, Stuff They Didn't Tell You

Do you think my kids are Y's? You bet they are!! The only time I've seen my oldest son act like an N is on the golf course. If you are a golfer you know that doesn't count.

Another interesting characteristic of Type N's is that they often feel compelled to talk to themselves out loud. My father used to do it all the time. It is not unusual to hear an N shouting questions to an empty room:
- "Why do these things only happen to me?"
- "Why does everything have to be "triple-hard"?" (obvious reference to the principle of Maximum Effort, discussed in Chapter Five)
- "Why is it that yesterday I had a dozen of them but today, when I need just one, there are none to be found?"
- "How could I have spilled that container that I deliberately put out of the way where I wouldn't spill it?"
- "Why does the car ahead of me refuse to turn left on a yellow light?"
- "Why do traffic jams always occur when I am late for an appointment?"
- "When I put something valuable in a special place where it won't get lost, why can't I find it the next day?"
- "Why is my poker hand always second best?" (see Chapter Twelve).

Actually, talking to one's self is often part of an N's attempt at remaining sane in a seemingly insane world (see Chapter Nine)

Almost all mechanics and technicians are Y's, especially those who work on commercial airplanes (I hope). If they weren't the daily frustration of fixing other peoples problems would kill them. That's why your family car makes that "something expensive is broken" sound when you drive it, but purrs like a kitten when the mechanic at the repair shop takes it for a test drive. He is a Y; of course it's going to run just fine for him. It only makes that sound when you drive it because you're an N. In fact Y's and N's seem to be more successful in certain professions. Let's look a few of these.

More Type Y people seem to wind up in the following jobs:
- Automobile mechanic

Newton & Einstein, Stuff They Didn't Tell You

- Computer Repair Technician
- Professional Golfer
- Professional Basketball Player
- Race Car Driver
- Airplane Pilot
- Brain Surgeon
- Hedge Fund Managers

The process of natural selection has weeded out the N's who ever tried to succeed in these professions. They either starved to death or switched to a different career path, if they survived. Auto mechanics and computer technicians lose their customers if they can't find what's wrong and fix it quickly. And you don't get many "do-overs" in professional sports, race car collisions, airplane crashes, or botched brain surgeries. Hedge Fund Managers? I'll leave that one for you to figure out.

Type N's find themselves in the following jobs:
- Shoe salesperson (e.g., Al Bundy)
- Computer Software Designer
- Lawyer
- Dermatologist
- Tax Auditor
- Meteorologist
- Quality Inspector
- Highway Patrolman
- Crisis Management Planner
- Government Project Design Contractor

Type N's can be successful in these professions because they get paid regardless of the outcome and they usually get multiple chances to get it right. Lawyers get paid whether they win or lose your case. And the quality of products being inspected never impacts the Quality Inspector's performance rating. I'm not saying that N's are less competent than Y's. The problem is that N's have to find those subtle mistakes that Mother Nature has embedded in their work (see

Newton & Einstein, Stuff They Didn't Tell You

Chapter Seven). Sometimes this takes several tries; one more thing Y's don't have to deal with.

To be fair, there is one profession that isn't in either list but could be in both. That profession is farming.

I recall the farmer who won $10 million in the lottery. The newspaper reporters asked what he planned to do with all the money. "Keep on farming until it's all gone", he immediately replied. This man was obviously an N who found a way to survive as a farmer. Farmers depend upon the weather and other uncertainties more than almost any other profession. Mother Nature can crush them like a bug anytime she feels like it. Obviously 99% of farmers who are successful must be Y's. In fact some are successful enough that the government pays them not to grow crops any more (i.e., no investment and no risk of crop failure). Name another profession where you get paid not to practice your chosen profession.

It is a fact that N's make excellent planners because they are accustomed to dealing with unexpected results.

Type N's learn to always have a "Plan B" ready in case "Plan A" fails, which it usually does. The really good planners even have "Plan C" and "Plan D", etc. For example, you would expect a Type N travel agency who plans your vacation itinerary to predict that the airline will lose all your luggage for the first four days of your five-day trip. Therefore, this travel agency's vacation package includes having a portion of your wardrobe sent to your hotel via overnight express mail, and a 24/7 emergency phone number for "Clothes R Us" in case overnight express delivers to the wrong hotel.

Can a Type Y change to a Type N?

I know of no recorded cases where a Y actually changed (permanently) to an N. Of course that may be because all Y's exposed to such a transition died prematurely, with their deaths attributed to heart attack or stroke. The sudden shock of that much frustration without time to adjust would be too much for anyone. Can a Y experience brief periods where he behaves like an N? The

Newton & Einstein, Stuff They Didn't Tell You

problem here is that, being a Y, the experience would need to last for more than a day or two to really be noticed. And then, fearing the transition is permanent, the Y would be in the situation discussed above.

Can a Type N change to a Type Y?

Such a transition is theoretically possible. However, one would expect to see newspaper headlines and I haven't seen any. Can an N experience brief periods where it seems like he is a Y? The answer to this one is definitely yes. As mentioned in a later chapter, such occasions should be embraced like winning the lottery (this is a close as an N will ever get). But don't expect it to last. Mother Nature doesn't stay distracted for long. She's going to notice you've strayed away from the flock and herd you back in again before long.

Is the number of Y's in the universe (or at least the Earth) increasing faster than the number of N's?

Based on Darwin's Theory of Evolution (struggle for survival and survival of the fittest) you might expect that the number of Y's would grow while the N's would eventually become extinct. However, much like the crew of the Starship Enterprise, Mother Nature has a "Prime Directive". That "Prime Directive" is to maintain the balance between those who get what they expect (Type Y's) and those who learn to expect what they get (Type N's).

By providing us N's with endless opportunities to learn survival skills that the Y's don't need, she avoids (or at least postpones) our extinction. Examples of survival skills we N's are forced to learn include:
- Almost infinite patience with anything mechanical or electronic
- Slowness to anger in the face of adversity and frustration
- Significantly enhanced ability to cope with the unexpected
- Compulsion to develop and research alternatives, even when there is no apparent need for them
- Preference for "thinking outside the box" (vs. conventional solutions that only work for Y's)
- Talent for invention during a crisis

Newton & Einstein, Stuff They Didn't Tell You

In summary, Type N's are forced to be more patient, more inventive, and more questioning of the world around them. That is how they survive.

Women aren't really smarter than men; it's just that more of them are Y's (in spite of not having the Y chromosome). It's one more edge they have over us men. This is why women can program a TV digital recorder and men can't? Fortunately men can now purchase DVD's that cover an entire season of their favorite TV program; this allows them to avoid the whole digital recording embarrassment thing. Why should there be a gender bias? Why are there more male N's and more female Y's? Obviously it's because Mother Nature is female. [One of Mother Nature's best jokes was to give the Y chromosome to men.]

Women directly control part of the wealth of the world, and simultaneously control the men who control the remainder.

This shouldn't come as a surprise. Women are skilled at multitasking. They can talk on the phone and cook at the same time. They can skillfully apply mascara (using the rearview mirror) while driving down the highway at 70 miles per hour. They can plan a banquet for thirty people while having sex and their husband never knows the difference. Women enjoy Mother Nature's little pranks, particularly when they happen to men. A damaged ego is always worth celebrating. Why shouldn't Mother Nature be on their side? They share a common agenda. It's mutual admiration, pure and simple.

Type N's are victimized by Mother Nature often enough that they consciously resent her interference in their lives. (If fact, that's another way we know we are N's!) They frequently observe evidence of the special physical laws described in this book, even if they don't' always understand what they see. Newton and Einstein may have been Type N's and decided to do the intelligent and noble thing by sparing the rest of us the ugly truth.

Since I am neither noble nor as smart as they were, here it comes.

Newton & Einstein, Stuff They Didn't Tell You

Chapter Three
The Nature of Mother Nature

It's important to remember that there are limits to what Mother Nature can do. If she goes too far you might establish proof of her interference in your life, and that would ruin the fun.

The limits of what she can do derive from the basic nature of Mother Nature. She is mischievous, but not to the point of directly causing you physical harm (e.g., something you could prove). In fact, Mother Nature is prohibited from directly causing physical pain or death. It's against her nature. So if you expect this book to explain why children die of cancer or why good people get injured in car accidents, you can stop reading now. You need to find a different book.

It is true that N's occasionally harm themselves out of frustration when it's a really bad day and they are losing the fight. But Mother Nature sees to it that you always retain the element of "free choice".

It was your decision to apply a little extra force to that screwdriver – not something you can clearly blame on her. In the movie "Bedazzled" (the original with Dudley Moore) you may recall all the pranks that Satan played on innocent people just to irritate them. Such things do actually happen, but it's not Satan who's at work here. Satan is much too busy with global terrorism, pedophilia in the Catholic Church, and other important stuff. He wouldn't take time to interfere with your life or mine in such childish ways. No, it's Mother Nature doing it. She isn't concerned with winning souls – she just likes to have fun at our expense. It's her job; it's what she does!

One more analogy is worth remembering; "Fighting against Mother Nature is like mud wrestling with a pig – you both get dirty and the pig likes it!"

It would not be fair to portray Mother Nature as the primary reason why bad things happen to those who don't deserve it. Most of the N's I know are in good

Newton & Einstein, Stuff They Didn't Tell You

heath, enjoy rewarding relationships with their family and friends, and have a reasonably affluent life style. N's don't seem to die of heart disease more frequently than Y's, or suffer physically or financially just because they are N's. Mother Nature is childish and petty, but not vindictive or cruel. It's just that being an N means Mother Nature likes to mess with you, to interfere in your life daily, to irritate you to the edge of madness anytime she can get away with it.

She also has one other annoying habit. While she is making your life miserable, she arranges for the Y's to witness your suffering as both incredibly pathetic and funny as hell. An N's life is the perfect fodder for those Y dominated cocktail parties. "Did you hear what happened to .... Can you believe it?!"

Many people associate Mother Nature with animals and wildlife, which exist in peaceful harmony with their environment. She is often portrayed as their friend and protector. It's clear she likes them better than people. We'll talk later about how that affects your chances as a hunter or fisherman. So why should Mother Nature favor non-humans over humans? The surface of planet Earth has been changed more in the last 3000 years by man than by all the animals for hundreds of millions of years before. Maybe Mother Nature liked things the way they were.

Despite all the entertainment we (with our emotions) provide her, my guess is that Mother Nature would be happier if evolution had skipped right over us humans and allowed dolphins, elephants or cockroaches to become the dominant species.

Mother Nature loves electronic stuff.

If you think about it for just a moment you can see why. Before the age of electronics every tool or gadget we used was mechanical. The nice thing about something mechanical is that when it stops working you can simply take it apart and see what is broken. The broken piece is right there in plain sight. My dad could fix anything in the house that stopped working, using only a screwdriver, a pair of needle nose pliers, and a quick trip to the local hardware store. When we began to use electronic tools and gadgets we lost that ability to see what is

Newton & Einstein, Stuff They Didn't Tell You

broken.

When your television, mobile phone or laptop computer stops working, taking it apart and looking for the broken piece doesn't work. In fact, simply looking inside usually voids the warranty, which lets the manufacturer off the hook for the cost of the repairs. By the way that is another of Mother Nature's little tricks. She and the manufacturer love it when they can get you to void your warranty protection. Electronic stuff gives Mother Nature a much wider range of options for making stuff not work in ways no one can explain. Her ability to frustrate all of us has been increasing exponentially since the electronics age began.

Frustration (yours) is Mother Nature's honey. It's what she lives for. And she remembers what aggravates you the most.

One of her favorites is to set you up for a minor disaster, leaving a subtle clue that it's coming. An experienced N can sense when this is happening. For example, if you are cooking and have very limited counter space. You turn to put down that bowl of whatever you are mixing and notice that there is only one place to put it. If you are an experienced N, you know what's next. Somehow in the next few minutes your elbow will hit that very bowl spilling the contents over you, the counter, the floor and everything else within reach. Obviously it's all because of where you put the bowl a few minutes before. But you didn't have a choice about where to put it did you? If you are an N you know Mother Nature just set you up, even though you can't prove it.

Mother Nature loves to mess with something mathematicians call the "Drunk Man Theory". The Drunk Man Theory says that if you stand a drunken man (i.e., someone only capable of random movement) on a white line in an empty parking lot, he will take his first step either to the right of the white line or to left. The theory argues that if he steps to the right of the line, it is very likely he will continue to stumble around on the right side for some time before he accidentally crosses the white line to the left side. Conversely, if the drunken man initially steps to the left of the line, then he will continue for some time on the left side before accidentally crossing the line to the right side.

Newton & Einstein, Stuff They Didn't Tell You

In a fair world and after a long time has passed we all expect to find that the drunken man has accumulated about the same amount of time on the right side of the white line as on the left. What this means is that bad luck usually continues for a while before it changes to good, and good luck will continue for a while before changing to bad. There are professional gamblers who rely on this theory to make a living. Here's where Mother Nature has her fun. For the Y's of the world, she leaves things just as I described above. The Y's have an even chance every morning to have a good day or a bad day.

But Mother Nature has it in for the N's.

After some years the N's begin to notice that they are spending a lot more time on one side of the white line than on the other. One theory is that Mother Nature moves the white line whenever it suits her, much like Lucy liked to pull the football away just as Charlie Brown was about to kick it in the famous Charles Shultz cartoon strip.

And just like Charlie Brown, we N's fall for it over and over again.

However she does it, N's don't start each day with an even chance.

The service department is always busy when an N calls. The Highway Department's computers are down the day they took off to renew their driver's license. The DVD player they bought doesn't work like the manual says and has to be "replaced or repaired at the manufacturer's convenience". (N's learn to read warranties – we use them a lot more than the Y's.) If you happen to have studied mathematics and have some sense of probabilities, it can be truly fascinating to be an N. It is like knowing the end of a mystery movie ahead of time.

You know that no matter how high your odds of success, and no matter how many alternate plans you have, Mother Nature will find some way to stop you from succeeding. Remember she controls the odds and can make anything happen as long as there is any chance at all. To observe how this occurs, all just barely within the bounds of random probability, can be really amazing.

Newton & Einstein, Stuff They Didn't Tell You

That's where those special physical laws come in handy. Mother Nature uses them to circumvent the normal probabilities that the Y's take for granted.

Newton & Einstein, Stuff They Didn't Tell You

Chapter Four
Special Physical Laws I

Truth is ever to be found in simplicity, and not in the multiplicity and confusion of things – Isaac Newton

Mother Nature uses special laws of physics (the ones Newton/Einstein didn't mention) to have her fun with those of us who happen to be Type N people.

In this chapter I'll describe these physical laws, and show how Mother Nature uses them to make us N's miserable. It is important to note that here again there are limitations. Mother Nature cannot contradict Newton's physical laws in ways that we can directly observe (and therefore prove). For example, Mother Nature cannot use the special law of Mischievous Attraction (described below) to make a ball roll up hill against the force of gravity. (I plan to get a government research grant to study this one if she ever tries it.) [Actually, we now know that gravity is nothing more than the mass of planet Earth warping time, changing our velocity into acceleration, which causes us to feel a force acting downward]. She can only use these special laws where random chance provides sufficient cover for her mischief.

Those of you with some knowledge of Chaos Theory and the "butterfly effect" will realize that, given enough opportunity, not much is outside her reach.

MN Law No. 1 – Mischievous Attraction

Arguably the most obvious of Mother Nature's special physical laws is the law of Mischievous Attraction. We'll refer to this one as MN Law No. 1.

No, we're not talking here about magnetism or the fact that your 16 year-old daughter has fallen madly in love with the 22 year-old son of a notorious drug dealer. Mother Nature can endow certain objects with a special property, which

Newton & Einstein, Stuff They Didn't Tell You

we will call Mischievous Attraction. Think of this special property as being like the force of gravity, only for much smaller objects than the moon, the planets, and your mother-in-law. If it helps, you can use Newton's formula, $F = MA$ (Force equals Mischievous Attraction). The best way to describe Mischievous Attraction is through several familiar (to us N's) examples.

If you own a canister vacuum cleaner you know that when you pull on the hose the canister part never rolls in the direction you are pulling. Instead it rolls toward the nearest obstacle, such as table leg or door facing so as to get itself into position to block your pull. This forces you to lay down the wand and hose portion and go dislodge the canister part out from behind whatever is holding it. Mother Nature can achieve a lot in this simple situation. First she forces you to stop vacuuming so as to prolong an unpleasant task you didn't really want to do anyway. Second she forces you to lay down the wand and hose creating an opportunity for you to tangle your feet or something else in the hose, which could lead to more fun. Third, she forces you to keep a watchful eye on the canister while you continue vacuuming so it doesn't get caught behind something again, which creates new opportunities for you to suck something up into the vacuum that you didn't intend.

Mother Nature refers to this scenario as a "three-for-one special". And all it takes is for the canister vacuum cleaner to acquire the property of Mischievous Attraction. In fact, Mother Nature ensures that all canister vacuum cleaners purchased by N's come so equipped.

Mother Nature applies the law of Mischievous Attraction to other things as well. Take, for example, a wire coat hanger in your closet. The problem is that (like potato chips) you can't take just one. If you try you will invariably get at least two or three because these things grab on to each other (i.e., Mischievous Attraction). Although a coat hanger has only one "hook", it behaves like the "grappling hooks" used to scale castle walls in the ninth Century. Trying to pull just one empty wire coat hanger out of the closet is sure to result in one or more entanglements. Struggling only results in your clean clothes landing on the floor.

In summary, closets are for hanging up your clothes, and also for hanging up

Newton & Einstein, Stuff They Didn't Tell You

wire coat hangers in each other if you try to remove just one at a time.

Plastic trash bags are another good example. When you open the box of plastic trash bags you are usually only interested in removing one. But the law of Mischievous Attraction ensures that you will get at least two or more. And it isn't because the manufacturer puts the bags into the box in pairs. I've actually cut open the box to be sure. You want to pull out just one bag, but you get two or three, so you have to stuff the extra ones you didn't want back into the box. This let's Mother Nature employ another of her special laws (principle of Maximum Effort), which will be discussed later.

Nowadays we also have plastic grocery bags (although these are being discouraged these days for sound environmental reasons) instead of those brown paper grocery bags that made good liners for the cat box or the floor of your canary cage.

With the paper bags you could remove your groceries with one hand and put them in the cupboard or refrigerator with the other hand. They also folded up nicely for storage. Not true for the plastic grocery bags. You've probably noticed that the plastic bags cling to the items inside and refuse to stand with their mouths open like the paper bags did. That means you need two hands to remove whatever is inside, one hand to grasp the item and the other to peel the bag away from it. Clearly Mischievous Attraction is at work here. And when you are done you are left with a pile of these plastic bags all over the floor just waiting to attach themselves to your feet, possible causing a nasty fall. Decades ago stores used to offer you a choice of paper or plastic bags for your groceries, but now it's up to each of us to bring our own permanent bags, and to sack our own groceries as well.

Next let's talk about those occasions when we drop something important.

The law of Mischievous Attraction holds that when you drop an object of significant value anywhere near an open hole, the object will most likely go into the hole. The more valuable the object and the deeper the hole, the greater the

Newton & Einstein, Stuff They Didn't Tell You

force exerted on the object to make it go into the hole. If fact, the relative size of the hole doesn't seem to matter much.

So let's examine this one mathematically. Let's assume that we are working with the world's supply of an extremely rare and hard to produce radioactive isotope. The capsule containing this material is one inch in diameter. And let's say that you intend to lower it on a cable down a 1000-foot drill hole that is three inches in diameter. Now the area you are working over is ten feet square. If we do some simple calculations, we find that the working area is 100 square feet, whereas the area of the hole is only about 0.05 square feet. So if we should happen to drop our one-inch diameter isotope source on the ground it has about one chance in 2000 of falling into the three-inch diameter hole, that is if we neglect the force created by the law of Mischievous Attraction.

As you've probably guessed by now, the MA force was so great in this case that when the isotope source was accidentally dropped it made the most amazing "hole-in-one" anyone had ever witnessed. It took some equally amazing feats of engineering almost a week to retrieve it.

Maybe you don't happen to have the world's supply of a rare radioactive isotope handy, but you would like to check out the MA force for yourself. Here are some things you can try at home.

Take a piece of jewelry like a diamond ring and drop in on the floor. If you are an N, the first thing that you will notice is that the item seems to have disappeared directly into the floor. Rest assured Mother Nature would never let that happen because then you would have proof that she interfered with your little experiment. No the item you dropped is still in the house. Start by looking under any furniture in the room or other locations where the item would be difficult to reach. If you really want to shorten the process, look first in the place that is most difficult to reach, like under the refrigerator. Odds are (thanks to Mother Nature) that is where you will find your jewelry.

Now if you do some simple calculations like we did before you will note that

Newton & Einstein, Stuff They Didn't Tell You

there should be a much higher probability that your jewelry would end up on the open floor somewhere in plain sight (or on your foot if the item you drop is heavy). After all there is much more open floor area compared to that covered by furniture. So why did your jewelry end up under the refrigerator? Simple! Mother Nature uses the MA force to make your life more interesting whenever possible. Count on it!

By the way, if any of you find your jewelry lying out on the open floor after you drop it, there is really no point in you reading the rest of this book. You are obviously one of Mother Nature's favorite Y's who leads a charmed life. You have better things to do, starting with putting an end to world hunger, global terrorism and violence in the Middle East.

Here are some more examples of how the law of Mischievous Attraction can affect your life if you are an N:

- Screws and pencils always roll off the table, even though the table is perfectly level.
- Any liquid spilled on your desk will immediately run toward your most important documents, and/or your most expensive electronics.
- Car doors swing wider when they are parked next to your car in the parking lot, and their paint doesn't match yours.
- You find your car traveling sideways down an icy street, which happens to be lined with parked BMW's and Mercedes.
- You stare at a spoon of ice cream as you hold it over the bowl waiting for the dangling part to drop off; finally you give up and watch it fall instead on your new cashmere sweater while in route from the bowl to your mouth.
- You're on vacation in France, half of your medication spills down the bathroom drain, and the doctor said to be sure and take all the pills or the infection could come back.
- A large pine tree surrounded by an empty field snaps and falls during a storm. It doesn't fall toward the north, or northeast, or east, or southeast, or south, or southwest, or west. It falls precisely northwest onto your boat parked 30 feet away.

Newton & Einstein, Stuff They Didn't Tell You

- More than any other substance in the universe, white carpet exhibits Mischievous Attraction, especially for red wine.
- You drop a sheet of paper. As you bend down to pick it up you discover it is stuck to the floor. Why? Because your foot is on it. You haven't moved either of your feet, so how did that happen??

Newton & Einstein, Stuff They Didn't Tell You

MN Law No. 2 – Malicious Repulsion

At first the law of Malicious Repulsion sounds simply like the antithesis of the law of Mischievous Attraction. Actually it is something quite different. The only thing these two laws really have in common is that energy is required in both cases and you never get what you want.

For example, with Malicious Attraction an expensive item dropped near a hole will almost always fall in, whereas Malicious Repulsion guarantees a golf ball that you are trying to putt into the hole will go anywhere but.

Centuries ago Isaac Newton observed that energy is required to move an object at rest, or to change the direction of an object already in motion. One century ago Albert Einstein proposed his famous equation relating energy to matter: $E = MC^2$. Energy equals mass times the speed of light (about 186,000 miles/second) squared. Nuclear fission can release huge amounts of energy from a relatively small amount of matter, as demonstrated first in the New Mexico desert, and later at various locations around the world. But if huge amounts of energy can be released from small amounts of matter, why can't very small amounts of energy (e.g., enough to change the roll of a golf ball) be released without noticing the change in mass of the golf ball?

Let's look at more specific examples in detail.

We have all noticed that sometimes a golf ball will roll around the lip of the hole and come back out going in a completely different direction. It turns out that the ball has to strike the lip of the cup at precisely (within a few millimeters) the right location and be traveling at precisely the right velocity to make this happen. Yet we see it happen many times during the average golf tournament. How can this be? The answer is that Mother Nature can extract tiny amounts of energy from the golf ball to make "lip-outs" happen as many times as she wants and no one can prove that it wasn't random. She can also make the ball suddenly curve to the left or right of the hole to avoid going in. Weighing the golf ball before

Newton & Einstein, Stuff They Didn't Tell You

and after these events won't help because the change in mass is just too small to notice.

Mother Nature loves games like golf, basketball and billiards for exactly that reason.

Actually, you don't even have to play golf, basketball or billiards to put Malicious Repulsion to the test, especially if you work in an office and have a few minutes to kill. (WARNING: This exercise may become addictive, especially if you are an N.)

Just put your trash can in one corner of the room or cubicle and proceed to toss wadded up sheets of paper at it. You will soon notice that a significant number of paper wads bounce off the rim of the trash can, sometimes even twice. Now if you calculate the area of the mouth of the trash can and compare it with the area represented by the rim of the trash can, you will notice that the probability must be very high that the paper wad will go into the can or miss the can entirely. To put it another way, you would not expect the paper wad to land on the rim very often.

So why does the paper wad hit the rim so often? Is the rim of the trash can displaying Mischievous Attraction or is the mouth of the can displaying Malicious Repulsion?

The answer is both. This is one of those occasions when Mother Nature can get you coming and going, literally! (Note: If you want an even more amazing experience, use a trash can that is round. This leaves a very small triangular space between the walls that form the corner of the room and the rounded edge of the trash can. Now toss your paper wad and watch it go directly into the tiny space between the walls and the trash can. You know that you couldn't do that deliberately in a thousand tosses. Yet it happens by accident. Amazing!)

Professional golfers, basketball players and pool sharks are some of Mother Nature's favorite Y's.

Newton & Einstein, Stuff They Didn't Tell You

If they weren't Y's they would soon starve to death. However, every once in a while Mother Nature will even play a trick or two on one of these people just for fun. Ever notice how even expert pool players will sometimes shoot the last ball for the win, then watch the ball rattle back and forth in the mouth of the pocket. It just sits there, refusing to drop. Or a pro golfer can win the PGA Championship one weekend, and then the next weekend he can't hit a fairway or sink one short putt out of ten? He tells the News Media he was just having a bad weekend (or month, or year!). Mother Nature knows better. She decided this guy was getting a little overconfident and it was time for her to remind him who's boss.

We N's just play golf because we are masochists. We also enjoy shopping for new golf clubs to replace the ones we tossed into the lake last weekend.

If you have ever stood at the kitchen sink rinsing off the dishes before putting them in the dishwasher you undoubtedly noticed another example of Malicious Repulsion. Water runs over the dishes and then down the drain in the center of the sink. So why doesn't it carry the food particles to the drain as well? You spray the water first on one side of the sink and then the other. The water goes down the drain but the food particles just move from one side of the sink to the other, refusing to follow the water down the hole in the middle. In fact you may even notice the food particles making their way up the sidewalls of the sink, as though they were alive and trying to escape from the sink altogether. This is the closest I have come to proving Mother Nature's interference with the laws of gravity. I haven't been able to capture this 'particle climbing' process on film just yet, but someday I will.

Brushing bread crumbs or trash off the sofa is yet another simple example. Observe how the harder you brush toward the edge of the sofa, the more the little pieces bounce in a direction opposite from the direction you are brushing. In fact, you can actually make them go further and further away from you simply by brushing them toward you. This actually works quite well with any upholstered furniture, the seats in your car, etc. Of course if you have leather

Newton & Einstein, Stuff They Didn't Tell You

seats in your car, you don't need to worry about getting trash out of them, other than the occasional blind date your sister keeps setting you up with.

When you are making the bed and you toss the sheet into the air over the bed, notice how the sheet always falls toward the right or left side, but never evenly on both sides, even though that is how you tossed it. Some people will explain this phenomenon by pointing to slight variations in the sheet, or the tossing of it, causing the air underneath to escape preferentially toward one side or the other. This causes the sheet to slide toward one side of the bed as it falls (i.e., the "butterfly affect"). Actually, this is just one more example of Malicious Repulsion. If you don't believe it, try a little experiment. Toss the sheet as many times as you like. Even though there is some chance it will land evenly at least once in a while, in fact it never lands evenly no matter how many times you try.

Of course if you happen to be a Type Y, this experiment won't work for you. But then you probably have someone who makes your bed for you, right?

One more example is particularly annoying. It involves garbage bags that get full and have to be set on the kitchen floor before you carry them out. I'm sure you've noticed that a bag of garbage is always heavier on one side than the other. Of course you don't want the bag to fall over and spill its contents onto the kitchen floor so you lean the bag against the cabinet or wall, taking great care to place the bag with the heavier side toward the wall. In theory this should be a stable position and the bag won't fall over.

If you are an N you know what happens next. As soon as you turn your back or leave the room, the bag falls over in spite of your thoughtful placement. You return to find garbage all over the floor. Once again Malicious Repulsion has done its thing. Your spouse, who is a Y, just can't understand how you could be so careless. What she does understand is that taking out the garbage is your job, not her's.

There's one more example of Malicious Repulsion (or maybe it's Mischievous Attraction in this case) that is worth mentioning.

Newton & Einstein, Stuff They Didn't Tell You

If you have more than a few pictures on your walls at home or at the office, you may have noticed from time to time that they get crooked and have to be straightened. Did the walls and the floor suddenly shift? Was there an earthquake that made the pictures move? Did someone deliberately push the pictures to the right or left (at least no one will admit it if they did)? Usually there is no rational explanation. It has to be one of those forces that Newton and Einstein didn't discover or chose not to talk about.

Newton & Einstein, Stuff They Didn't Tell You

MN Law No. 3 – Irrational Resistance

We all experience friction in our lives.

I'm not talking about disagreements we have with family members or coworkers. I'm talking here about things that slide on one another, like ice skates on a frozen lake; and things that shouldn't slide, like your tires on wet pavement. Engineers use the term "coefficient of friction" to explain why some things slide easily and some don't. In a rational world slippery things like Teflon have a low coefficient of friction, and other things like pine resin have a high coefficient of friction.

Now let's talk about the irrational world that us N's live in.

Anything that screws together can serve as a good example of friction that's out of control. Take your average nut and bolt. Screwing a nut onto a bolt should be easy, i.e., you can hand tighten until you reach the point where the nut is snug. Then it takes a wrench to tighten it further. That's how nuts and bolts are designed to work. But Mother Nature likes to change the way things work when it suits her. When that repair job has been long one and she has you pinned to the mat with her foot on your neck, she throws in something extra.

It's a 3 inch long bolt with a nut that is "tight all the way". That means instead of using a wrench to loosen and then removing the nut by hand, you have to use the wrench (or wrenches if the bolt head is free to turn) for every single turn of the nut for the entire length of the bolt. If clearances happen to be close (they always are), you won't be able to get a ratchet wrench to work, either. Amazing how slow and tedious those box end wrenches can be (the principle of Maximum Effort will be discussed later).

Another good example of irrational resistance is the zipper.

The zipper has to be one of Mother Nature's all time favorite inventions. Getting all those little teeth on the right side to neatly engage all their little counterparts on the left side is invisibly managed by (here's your first clue) the "Y shaped"

Newton & Einstein, Stuff They Didn't Tell You

thing you pull on. You guessed it. That "Y shaped" thing only works for Y's. The "Y shaped" thing instantly recognizes the pull of an N and jams up. The fun thing about zippers is that when they jam going forward, they almost always jam in reverse as well. And like pulling on a knot to loosen it, the more you struggle the more jammed the zipper becomes. Now you find yourself only partially dressed, unable to go forward or back. In general, society isn't very kind to people who go around only partially dressed. As a result, having a jammed zipper usually leads sooner or later to some form of social embarrassment.

And any form of social embarrassment simply makes Mother Nature's day!

But just because the zipper doesn't jam while you're getting dressed doesn't mean you're home free. Zippers have other failure modes. Sometimes, for no apparent reason, zippers unzip themselves without help from the "Y shaped" thing. While the "Y shaped" thing is safely at the top, all those little teeth simply disengage from the bottom up. Now is when you need the "Y shaped" thing to work upside down. Of course it won't do that. Once again some sort of social embarrassment is inevitable.

Y's love it when N's have wardrobe malfunctions.

Women (being favored by Mother Nature since they are the same gender) have at least found a partial solution to the zipper dilemma. Most clothes designed for women have the zippers in the back. That means that women can't be expected to zip up their own clothes. That is why they have husbands, boy friends, etc. Now when the zipper on their favorite dress jams, the husband, boy friend, etc. is obviously to blame. What men don't realize is that most women's clothing is designed with extra material behind the zipper so the clothes can be let out later in case the wearer gains a few unexpected pounds. It's usually that extra material getting caught in the zipper that actually causes it to jam.

See, it wasn't your fault after all.

Why do the people who make over the counter medicines insist upon putting a wad of cotton in the top of the bottle?

Newton & Einstein, Stuff They Didn't Tell You

They put it on top of the pills where you have to pull it out first before you can get to the medicine. The mouth of the bottle is too narrow to get your fingers in to grab the cotton, so you end up using a pencil, kitchen knife or whatever is available. Of course the cotton comes out in pieces so it takes you some time to get all the pieces out. Maybe you can get enough of it out to get to the medicine. In that case you can just leave part of the cotton in the bottle and say "to hell with it!"

I think the people that make over the counter medicines are secretly on Mother Nature's payroll.

Getting cookies out of the package without breaking them is another trip to Never-Never Land. I like to take all the cookies out of the bag and put them in a cookie jar where they will stay fresh. The cookies at the bottom of the bag are always broken by the time I get to them. Maybe they were already broken. I can't be sure. The point is that unless you are skilled surgeon and can perform a "Cesarean Section" to "deliver" the cookies unharmed, you just have to get used to eating broken cookies.

Rearranging furniture is a favorite pastime for many of us N's, because the person we live with says it is.

Coefficients of friction have been established for most types of carpet. Based on that information most pieces of furniture should just slide from where they are to where you (she) want them to be. If you are an N you know that pushing on furniture makes it tip over not slide, even when you push at a low point. The fact that someone had to invent these little plastic disks to put under your furniture legs is a clear indication that Mother Nature is alive and well.

Then there are those jar lids. You put them on without tightening so they will be easy to remove again. Only the next time to try to open one you'd swear it's been superglued. Jar lids and nails are close relatives in Mother Nature's family. Try pulling nails out of a board with a claw hammer or crowbar. Yep, more

Newton & Einstein, Stuff They Didn't Tell You

superglue. It's not unusual to pull the head off a nail instead of getting the nail out of the board, just to make the job a little harder.

Sometimes Mother Nature can combine her special laws for maximum impact.

Let's consider your household medicine cabinet, the one that contains nearly thirty bottles that should have been thrown out years ago. This morning you want that bottle of aspirin. In spite of the odds, you try to "surgically remove and replace" the bottle of aspirin without having all the other bottles fall out of the cabinet. Is this ever possible? No, because Mother Nature has everything going for her on this one.

Malicious Repulsion says that the bottle you try to remove will knock over at least two other bottles, which in turn will each knock over two other bottles, and so on. It all happens too fast for the human eye to follow. This is the same chain reaction that drives nuclear fission so there's no doubt it works. Mischievous Attraction says that all these medicine bottles would rather be on the floor of your bathroom anyway, preferably under and behind the toilet. And finally, the principle of Maximum Effort promises that you will spend 10 minutes picking up all those medicine bottles and putting them back in the cabinet vs. the 10 seconds you had intended to spend getting the aspirin.

Of course you can claim a small victory in this scenario if you pick up the bottles and put them in the trash rather than back in the medicine cabinet. But what fun would that be?

Some of our modern appliances come with electric cords that retract automatically or at least they're designed to. Vacuum cleaners are a prime example. Observe how many times you push the button and the cord doesn't retract all the way. Sometimes it ties itself in knots right in front of your eyes. Or maybe it gets itself wrapped around a table leg, a chair or your foot. Mother Nature likes to make things wrap around or under your foot because somehow you feel responsible.

It's must be your fault; you should have been standing somewhere else, right?

Newton & Einstein, Stuff They Didn't Tell You

Metal things are supposed to slide past each other but they don't. Try putting silverware into those little bins in the dishwasher. A simple fork grabs onto a nearby spoon, and trying to remove it brings three other utensils out onto the floor of the dishwasher where you have to remove the basket to reach them (see the principle of Maximum Effort again.) Generally speaking, anytime something should easily slide by something else but doesn't, you can bet it's Irrational Resistance in action.

The ultimate Irrational Resistance experience involves trying to put on a sweater over another sweater.

Admittedly, not even us N's often try this but if you do you're in for a treat. Some of the difficulties can be blamed on static electricity, but even that has its limits. Two materials acting like they are made of Velcro is what you've got. And no matter how hard you struggle, the chances of you looking or being comfortable are virtually nonexistent. Starting over is the only solution. Almost as much fun is putting on rubber gloves over rubber gloves (nuclear workers do this all the time).

Packing things in a bag can really test your patience. You carefully create a space in the bag that's large enough for that cell phone, digital camera, etc. But just before you place the item in the bag the other items close in. The space you made is gone. So you set the item down, carefully create the necessary space and try again. Remember Mother Nature loves repletion. Don't be surprised if you have to give up and pack the item somewhere else just to stop the madness.

For one last example of Irrational Resistance let us consider the famous "dotted line".

Everything is supposed to tear on the dotted line, but very few things actually do. Look at my checkbook. I do well to make sure the check number ends up with the check each time. I recall some airplane designers who were having problems with wing construction. Seems one wing kept tearing away from the fuselage

Newton & Einstein, Stuff They Didn't Tell You

during the wind tunnel tests. Finally one of them drew a dotted line with a magic marker right across the wing joint to the fuselage.

That solved the problem.

Newton & Einstein, Stuff They Didn't Tell You

Chapter Five
Special Physical Laws II

The next Special Physical Law has very broad applications. Mother Nature uses it primarily to ensure balance (according to her thinking) in the universe.

Just as Newton and Einstein insisted on mass and energy balances, so Mother Nature insists that there be a balance of negative and positive consequences. We usually refer to these as problems and solutions. Simply put, each time we solve a problem, the solution to that problem must generate at least one or more new problems needing to be solved.

MN Law No. 4 – The Law of Unintended Consequences

You may have noticed that the world is becoming increasingly more complex, requiring an ever-increasing number of problem-solvers to keep things running. More generally stated: Any action that produces a desired consequence will also result in one or more unwanted consequences, some being trivial and others more significant.

Here are a few examples of the law of unintended consequences:

- Importing the English Sparrow to control insect infestations, leading to a permanent infestation of English Sparrows in the North American Continent
- Introducing a beaver-like animal called a Nutria to control the growth of Lilly Pads in Louisiana wetlands, resulting in those wetlands being overrun by Nutria looking for food once all the Lilly Pads were gone
- Spraying pesticides over the rice patties in Beaumont, Texas to eradicate the dragonfly population, resulting in an explosion in the mosquito population (dragonflies eat mosquito larva)

Newton & Einstein, Stuff They Didn't Tell You

- Spending twenty years to develop better drugs for pain control, only to find out after they go on the market that they may cause heart problems
- Advanced pesticide applications to prevent insects from eating food crops, resulting in poisoning our natural water supplies
- Depleting this planet's natural ultraviolet radiation filter (ozone layer) by converting essentially all popular pump spray products to aerosol cans that use a propellant called Freon
- Inventing the business photocopier, resulting in our landfills being filled with millions of tons of waste paper products
- If you quit smoking, you gain weight (Did you lengthen your life or shorten it?).

Anytime you do something to improve one condition, you can expect your actions to set in motion a chain of events causing unwanted things to happen with slightly greater consequence. In fact if one were to collect the data, they would discover three subtle but basic truths about the Law of Unintended Consequences:

1. The number of unintended consequences of any action will always outnumber the intended consequences of that action by at least one (believe me those unintended consequences are there even though you may not see them right away).
2. This ensures that our world is inexorably trending toward an unintended configuration rather than toward an intended one.
3. No matter what the politicians promise you, they can't change No. 1 and No. 2.

It all has to do with something called "Entropy", which we'll talk more about later.

"Chaos theory", frequently referred to as the "butterfly effect" is Mother Nature's clever way of producing unintended consequences with no way to prove she was involved. It may not be intuitively obvious that a butterfly flapping its wings in Hong Kong can actually result in a hurricane in Florida. However, slight random variations that never repeat do occur in all physical processes. Mother Nature sees to it that these random variations occasionally influence the results in a significant way, making it impossible for us to be completely certain that these

Newton & Einstein, Stuff They Didn't Tell You

processes will work as intended every time. That means that just because you received 105 emails from your boss in the past month there is no guarantee you'll receive the 106th one, the one that says you need to be in Chicago on Monday morning.

When you recognize how over-dependent many of us have become on modern infrastructure (the internet, electricity, prepackaged food, pharmaceuticals, municipal water and sewer services, fuel for our cars, trains, planes, etc.), the opportunities for each of us to actually observe the "butterfly effect" are huge. Consider electric power grid failures that have occurred in the last few decades. Our electric power infrastructure has the following characteristics that make it ripe for Mother Nature's pranks, with a little help from "Chaos Theory":

- Distributed over a very large area, requiring many thousands of miles of cabling and circuitry
- Monitored and controlled by computers, because the system is too complex to operate manually
- Must respond to a diverse and varying electrical load controlled by millions of individuals and businesses switching on and off millions of appliances and machines at random
- Operating very close to maximum capacity much of the time, because excess capacity is expensive to build and maintain
- Managed from moment to moment by computer systems that periodically fail in ways that no one alive today can explain.

So Mother Nature decides one day to spill the bowl of popcorn that distracts the programmer who's writing the software upgrade that controls the electric power grid that lights the lights in four highly populated New England states. A few years later, when conditions favor the programmer's error, everything suddenly goes dark in New York, New Jersey, etc.

Headlines read "Popcorn Causes New England Blackout!" Mother Nature never seems to get the credit she deserves.

Whether you are an N or a Y, you make choices every day that affect the rest of your life. Some choices deserve considerable thought because the consequences

Newton & Einstein, Stuff They Didn't Tell You

of a wrong choice may be severe and/or irreversible. Other choices are easy and affect our lives only in trivial ways (as far as we know). Most of us can remember some instance where we made a choice that had an unforgettable unexpected outcome. I recall leaving the house for work one morning, then having to go back to retrieve a briefcase I had forgotten, making me a few minutes later than usual. That morning there was an accident at a dangerous intersection in my route to work. Several people were killed in a collision between an SUV and an eighteen-wheeler. Had I driven through that intersection when I normally do, I might well have been the vehicle hit by the eighteen-wheeler. My friends told me my "Guardian Angel" was looking out for me that morning.

In case you are wondering, Guardian Angels are much more powerful than Mother Nature.

The point is that we tend to judge the correctness of our decisions by the consequences we observe. Let's use the SUV, eighteen-wheeler accident as an example:
- My choice to go back and retrieve the briefcase that morning may have saved my life, (i.e., "correct choice")
- Suppose, however, I never saw or heard about the accident and my boss chewed me out for being late to work (i.e., "incorrect choice")

In both cases my choice was the same, only the consequences I observed were different.

If you've watched an American football game on TV you've probably witnessed another example. It's the last 30 seconds of the game and the quarterback throws to a receiver who is double covered. If the ball is caught, the TV commentators proclaim it a brilliant throw by one of the best quarterbacks to play the game. If the ball is intercepted, those same TV commentators are instantly critical of that same quarterback for making the biggest mistake of the game. The quarterback's action was the same in both cases, but the consequences were different.

Newton & Einstein, Stuff They Didn't Tell You

One of the things that sets Y's and N's apart is how they observe the consequences of their choices, and how those observations influence future choices they make.

Mother Nature uses the law of Untended Consequences to confuse us N's about the correctness of our decisions. It appears that to get what we want, we must also accept things we don't want. At the end of the day we tally up the "correct choices" and the "incorrect choices" based on whether getting what we wanted was worth all the things we got that we didn't want. It's like taking a handful of jellybeans from a jar. If you like the red ones but hate the yellow ones, then getting more red ones than yellow ones represents success. Mother Nature sees to it that Y's get more red ones, while N's get more yellow ones. Type Y's will be eager to grab another handful of jellybeans, while N's will ponder whether it's worth just getting more yellow jellybeans that they can't get rid of.

Newton & Einstein, Stuff They Didn't Tell You

MN Law No. 5 – Principle of Maximum Effort

Those with engineering backgrounds probably remember a term called "Entropy". In spite of the lack of any physical manifestation of Entropy, we engineering students accepted it as a measure of how mixed together everything is in the universe. It always takes energy to start with a bunch of stuff that is all mixed together and separate out one item in its pure form.

Mother Nature takes advantage of this fact to have some fun with us N's.

Have you ever noticed that when you drop something it always has enough energy to roll to a location just out of reach, or fall to a spot where it is very difficult to retrieve? In such cases Mother Nature is not satisfied with simply making you drop the item. She adds insult to injury by making you spend the maximum amount of effort possible to retrieve it. This is the principle of Maximum Effort. Entropy says that it takes energy to retrieve something in its pure form. The principle of Maximum Effort goes a step further. It says you have to spend as much energy as possible to achieve whatever goal you set.

Mother Nature's favorite tool for achieving maximum effort is repetition.

For example, consider the task of dressing your three-year-old to go outside and play in the snow. It's only after she is fully dressed that she tells you she needs to go to the toilet. Mother Nature just succeeded in making you undress her, wait for her to go, and then redress her all over again. Isn't repetition fun? But it can get worse. The fully dressed three-year-old who has to go to the toilet now has the zipper stuck on her parka. While you are trying to unstick the zipper, she decides she can't wait any longer. Since she has now wet all her clothes, you get to bath her and redress her from the skin out. By the time all this is accomplished the snow has melted and people are already talking about spring.

Mother Nature always favors the incorrect orientation on anything us N's have to deal with.

Newton & Einstein, Stuff They Didn't Tell You

Given free choice over a binary event we almost always orient things backwards the first time, even though the "normal" odds of getting it right should be 50/50.

Examples include:
- Polarized electric plugs and other devices with binary orientation (your first attempt is always backwards),
- [Have you ever tried to insert an electrical plug into a socket in the dark? Even though the slots in the socket are tapered you will find it is practically impossible. And the Braille system (i.e., using your fingers to guide the plug into the socket) is a good way to get electrocuted.]
- Socks and trouser-pockets (they are always inside out when you remove them from the drier no matter which way you put them in)
- Screwed fittings (they always cross thread on the first attempt),
- Screw drivers (you find a flat blade when you needed a cross-head, and vice versa)
- Units of Measure (you find a one-quarter inch socket wrench when you needed a 10 mm)
- Hot water handle for the shower in a hotel room (you always get the cold water handle, unless that is the one you wanted).

Remember the objective is to force you to spend as much energy as possible to make things work as intended. When your first choice is always wrong repetition is guaranteed. And repetition is the key to maximizing the effort needed to succeed.

In situations where there are more than two choices the first several selections will likely be incorrect; i.e., more repetition, more effort. You know Mother Nature is enjoying herself when you select the same incorrect item more than once (repeated repetition).

Newton & Einstein, Stuff They Didn't Tell You

Examples where this is likely include:
- Socket sets, Box-end wrenches and Allen wrenches (it's even more fun if you mix the Metric and English ones together),
- Lids for Tupperware and Rubbermaid containers (more fun again if you mix them together),
- Miscellaneous screws, nuts and bolts (all in the same coffee can, right?),
- Keys (all on the same key ring),
- Documents in a file drawer (they're all eight and one-half by eleven inches and the same color),
- Different flavors of soup, baby food, coffee, etc. on the grocery shelves (almost identical labels for different flavors)

One of my college professors was a close friend of Mother Nature. (I think they were roommates at summer camp one year.)

She used to have some fun with her engineering students by messing up the units on our exams. One of her exam problems expressed velocity in furlongs (220 yards) per fortnight (14 days), and density in stones (14 lbs) per firkin (9 gallons). It took more effort to get the problem into a workable set of units than to do the math. One student (obviously a young N) actually asked the professor what kind of stone, granite or quartz? This professor clearly understood how to apply the principle of Maximum Effort.

When you store things in a toolbox, drawer or cabinet you can bet that the item you go looking for will be at the bottom and in the back. Why couldn't it be on top in front? You just put it in there last week. Mother Nature guarantees that the items you use the most will always be at the bottom and in the back. If there are enough other things you don't want in the drawer or cabinet you will likely have to remove most of them to get to the item you want. And that's how the things you want end up on the bottom and in the back all the time.

This discussion also applies to women's purses, especially the big floppy kind that seem to hold everything but the kitchen sink. You ladies know what I'm talking about, right? Your favorite lipstick is always at the bottom and you can never find it without taking everything else out. I've seen you do this at restaurants. When the waiter brings the food, there's no place on the table to put it until you put all that stuff back in your purse.

Now you might think that Mother Nature is also responsible for the fact that everything the government buys seems to cost 10 times as much as when you or I buy the same thing. Actually that has nothing to do with Mother Nature or the principle of Maximum Effort. The out-of-control bureaucracy we call our federal government is wholly responsible for that.

Newton & Einstein, Stuff They Didn't Tell You

MN Law No. 6 – Non-Random Probability

If you are a Y, you've probably noticed that the phrase "Random Probability" seems redundant, like saying the Atlantic Ocean is wet. Of course probability is random; how could it be otherwise. Mother Nature has the answer.

If you are a Type N you have to make appropriate adjustments in the laws of probability.

For example, the odds of a coin toss landing either heads or tails is 50% if you are a Y. But if you are an N, the odds are only 33% that the coin will land whichever way you call it. Get together with another N some evening and check it out if you don't believe me! After about a thousand tosses you'll be convinced. The same is roughly true when betting on black or red at the roulette table. When it comes to betting on a particular number, playing blackjack, etc., the math becomes much too complicated to go into here.

Suffice it to say that all the textbooks on probability only apply to the Y's.

Mother Nature can exert a non-random influence on the weather (especially in England), but even with her talents, it's hard for her adversely affect only certain people's weather (the N's) and not everyone else's. Actually she doesn't have to make it rain on your outdoor wedding. She only has to persuade the weatherman to predict rain in your area. Once you've gone to the extra trouble and expense to protect against rain, it no longer matters whether it actually rains on your location or not.

In fact the language used by weather forecasters is designed to discriminate against the N's of the world.

For example, if the meteorologists forecast a 50% probability of thunderstorms in your area it actually means two things. For the Y's it means a 50% chance that any of them will see any rain at all that day. For the N's it means a 100% chance that half of them will get wet. You can see the difference. Meteorologists really

Newton & Einstein, Stuff They Didn't Tell You

can't lose (that why it's such a good profession for us N's). Every day according to someone somewhere the forecast prediction was correct.

What a great place for non-random probabilities to hide.

If you happen to be in the business of operating nuclear reactors, you put great faith in probabilities. We like to calculate the probability of a reactor accident based on the probabilities that individual safety systems might fail. We feel pretty safe if the chance of a serious reactor accident is calculated to be one in a million years. The problem is that we interpret that answer to mean that such an accident won't happen in our lifetime, when actually that "once in a million years" could be tomorrow. And in fact both the Three Mile Island reactor accident in Pennsylvania and the Chernobyl reactor accident in the Former Soviet Union (FSU) have happened in our lifetime.

I'm not saying that these facilities were operated by N's or that Mother Nature had a hand in either of these events. All I am saying is that even when probabilities are truly random, it's not as comforting as we would like. And when probabilities are non-random it's even worse.

For Type N's Mother Nature sees to it that the laws of chance are as much against you as she can get away with and not become obvious. I'll save the details of how Mother Nature's law of Non-Random Probability can profoundly affect every aspect of your life (if you are an N) until later in the book.

Newton & Einstein, Stuff They Didn't Tell You

MN Law No. 7 – A Twist in Time

One of Mother Nature's less spectacular (but still amazing) magic tricks is to mysteriously twist ropes, electrical cords, telephone cords, etc. into knots whenever these things are left unattended.

I returned from a week of vacation to find the cord between the receiver and the console of my telephone in my office was twisted into no less than three separate knots. My secretary confirmed that my office had remained locked during my entire absence. Of course Radio Shack sells these little gadgets that eliminate twisting in telephone cords. Mother Nature hates them. That's why when you go there to get one they are usually sold out.

Garden hoses are another good example of the Twist in Time phenomenon. Just try washing your car without spending most of your energy fighting the hose. Every time it twists itself into a knot it cuts off the water flow. That's the hose's way of demanding and getting your undivided attention. And you can't get the knot out by untwisting the hose from your end. No, you have to actually go and grab the knot itself and remove the kink.

Mother Nature has endowed garden hoses with memories. Once a hose knots itself in a particular location it remembers to knot itself over and over again in the very same place.

Back in the days before USB ports and wireless networks it took from five to a dozen cables to hook your computer to your printer, external hard drive, speakers, telephone line, router, etc. The family entertainment center was even worse. You needed cables between the TV and the satellite receiver or cable box, the digital recorder, the DVD player, the CD player, the stereo tuner/amplifier, and the speakers (five or more, if you had surround sound). And each of these devices also had its own electrical cord.

Mother Nature convinced electronics manufacturers that it would be more fun if each of these devises were built and sold separately. That way consumers could

Newton & Einstein, Stuff They Didn't Tell You

make any number of mistakes buying devices that were incompatible and then having to return them. It also helps sell those multiple-socket surge protectors.

I'm sure Mother Nature owns stock in the company that makes those things.

To their credit, manufacturers solved the incompatibility problems (the companies that didn't went out of business - remember Betamax videotape players?). But the idea of having to buy separate devices and hook them together with cables pretty much stuck. So Mother Nature won, at least temporarily. If you wanted to disconnect any single device from the rest, you could look forward to untangling that device's cables from all the others. The Twist in Time effect ensured that cables you carefully routed last month would be wrapped around one another a month later. Unplugging cables from devices you didn't want to disconnect was inevitable. Getting them all back correctly took endless patience. Nowadays many devices are wireless, greatly reducing the number of cables. But to get even, Mother Nature arranged for everything to depend on your router, a single point of failure than can take down all your electronics in the blink of an eye.

Boat manufacturers know all about the Twist in Time effect. That's why they provide cleats to wrap the mooring ropes around instead of expecting you to coil the ropes into a pile on the deck. Mooring rope cleats on a boat are like cup holders in a new car. Sales are made or lost because of such things.

Mother Nature enjoys the holidays, even though she never takes one herself.

Christmas is her favorite. That's when we drag all those boxes of stuff down from the attic. Those stands of garland and sparkly stuff have had all year to tie themselves in knots just for our enjoyment. And who could forget the Christmas tree lights. In a contest between untangling Christmas tree lights and untangling barbed wire, I'd take the barbed wire. I remember when a single burned out light would prevent an entire string of Christmas tree lights from burning. Those were the good old days. It could take hours to find the one bulb that was burned out.

Sometimes Mother Nature would make things more interesting by putting two

Newton & Einstein, Stuff They Didn't Tell You

burned out lights on the same string. That way no matter which bulb you replaced the lights wouldn't light. Of course us N's got wise to Mother Nature's pranks. We bought new Christmas tree lights (relying on the 90 day warranty) every year just to spite her.

Here are some more examples of how the Twist in Time phenomenon makes our lives more challenging:
- Hair dryer cords that knock over everything on your bathroom counter when you try to untwist them,
- Vacuum cleaner hoses,
- Bed sheets in the washing machine (if the agitator rotates clockwise, why are the bed sheets twisted into knots counterclockwise?),
- Airport landing patterns (some of these make the news),
- Tangled parachute lines (not many of these get reported).

I'll have a lot more to say about Mother Nature's special relationship with time in the next section and in Chapter Fifteen.

Newton & Einstein, Stuff They Didn't Tell You

MN Law No. 8 – Delayed Reaction

Once Mother Nature realizes you are on to her little tricks she begins to mix things up a bit just to throw you off.

For example an item you place on a table or the floor will appear to be stable and only fall after you turn away. It doesn't matter how long you watch and wait, the action you don't want only happens when your back is turned. She can delay the actions caused by any of the special laws discussed earlier if it works for her and against you. Obviously a spill that isn't noticed immediately will be more difficult and time consuming to clean up (principle of Maximum Effort).

Stated more generally, bad things don't happen while you are watching; they wait until you're not looking so as to maximize the consequences.

Here are some examples of how Mother Nature makes an N's life more challenging by adding delay to her little pranks:
- That expensive fountain pen you lost last week turns up in a shirt pocket after you just washed it and your other white clothes, which are now a strange shade of blue (N's learn to search their clothes before they're washed).
- That shutoff notice from the electric company gets delivered to the wrong address – you're watching the Superbowl when the lights go out.
- You run over a nail on a busy Interstate Highway but the tire doesn't actually go flat until you're on a back country road after dark.
- The second leg of your flight to Frankfurt, Germany is cancelled but you don't find out until you've completed the first leg from Denver to New York's Kennedy Airport.
- That SUV doesn't pull out in front of you until you take your eyes off the road to answer the phone,
- The caller doesn't tell you the bad news until after the crash.

Newton & Einstein, Stuff They Didn't Tell You

Chapter Six
Mind Games I

Nature does nothing in vain when less will serve; for Nature is pleased with simplicity and affects not the pomp of superfluous causes – Isaac Newton

Newton and Einstein explained the workings of the Cosmos, but they couldn't explain the human experience. Mother Nature likes to play mind games with us N's when she gets particularly bored. You Y's will no doubt swear I am making things up again, right?

MG No. 1 – Shell Game

Let's say you are trying to tighten that tiny screw that holds your glasses together. You need that jeweler's screwdriver set you bought last month for just such an occasion. It's right there in the kitchen drawer where you saw it just yesterday, right? Wrong! You only saw it there because you were looking for something else. Now that you actually need a jeweler's screwdriver set it's no longer there.

I call this the Shell Game because it resembles the popular con played by those suspicious looking people on city street corners. They show you the pea, place it under one of three shells, rearrange the shells and ask you to pick which shell contains the pea. Since you just saw the pea being placed under the shell you know exactly where the pea is. Only when the guy lifts the shell you picked, the pea isn't there.

Mother Nature does the same thing with whatever you happen to be looking for at the moment. The fact that you saw the item in question just a few days ago is all part of the con. Generally speaking, whatever you need is never where you

Newton & Einstein, Stuff They Didn't Tell You

put it or last saw it, but you will easily find everything you were searching for yesterday and no longer need. Tomorrow you will find the thing you were looking for today, after you give up and make do with something else, i.e., you no longer need the thing you finally found. Since Y's don't go through such experiences, they will have a hard time following this logic. But if you're an N you've been there many times.

Just remember that today is the tomorrow we talked about yesterday. See how simple?

Some of you may be old enough to remember a television game show called "Concentration". The object of this game was to have contestants call out pairs of numbers corresponding to squares on a big game board. As each pair of numbers was called, those two squares would turn to reveal prizes that could be won. If two squares showed the same prize, the squares would turn further to reveal portions of a puzzle that the contestants had to solve. If the prizes didn't match, the two squares would turn back to their original positions revealing nothing of the puzzle, and the other contestant would take their turn.

The way to win the game was to "concentrate" and remember what prizes were under each of the numbers so you could make a match on your turn. When you made a match you got that prize added to your potential winnings and you got one guess at solving the puzzle, from what you could see of it. The more matches, the more of the puzzle you could see, and the easier it was to guess the solution for a win. Obviously contestants in this game had to have good short-term memories. And that's where Mother Nature steps in. She tricks us N's into remembering something that never happened – thinking we saw something we really didn't. Then when we go there to get that something it seems to have disappeared. How do I know she didn't actually move the thing we are looking for? Because that is something you could prove.

Remember Mother Nature likes to mess with your head, but do something you can prove? Not a chance. Fortunately she only messes with our short-term memories. My dad at age 85, for example, couldn't remember what he bought at the grocery store yesterday, but he could recite poems his grandmother taught

Newton & Einstein, Stuff They Didn't Tell You

him when he was ten years old. As I've gotten older this strange behavior has gradually become less and less mysterious. More on that in Chapter 19.

The Shell Game also works with your favorite jewelry (earrings, broaches, etc.), especially if you are already late getting dressed and don't have much time to look for the only ear rings that go with the new outfit you bought just for tonight. Women's shoes can play the game too.

The Shell Game actually has one rule that is worth remembering.

If you find what you are looking for, it will be in the last place you look. Now we've all heard this trick phrase since we were children; of course it is in the last place you look because when you find it you stop looking! But for N's it's a bit different. If an N finds what he is looking for, it will be in the last place he CAN look. For example, if there are five possible places to look for a particular thing you will find it in the fifth place you look. If there are ten possible places to look, you will find your missing item in the tenth place you look.

If there are forty possible places to look spread out over Texas, New Jersey, Montana, Florida and Maine, you will have to visit all five states before you find your missing item. It all goes back to the Principle of Maximum Effort we talked about in Chapter Five.

We N's sometimes think we can outsmart Mother Nature when something is lost, but she is just too clever. If we start looking in the place least likely to be hiding our item, she plants it in the most likely place. If we start looking in the most likely place, she hides it in the least likely place. If we consciously disregard the most likely and least likely places, and simply start looking at random, she still manages to put the lost item in the last of all possible locations.

Mother Nature loves to play the Shell Game with us at the Shopping Mall.

In fact, shopping is a lot like playing the game of Concentration, which includes remembering where in the Mall parking lot you parked your car. If you are an N

Newton & Einstein, Stuff They Didn't Tell You

and you find something you want at the Mall, just buy it. In fact buy two or three. Mother Nature knows the things you like and arranges for the company to stop making them. Or she simply changes the package so you don't recognize the product any more. Or some larger company merges with the original manufacturer so the name of the product changes. Grocery stores, discount stores, and pharmacies like to wait until you learn where your favorite products are. Then they rearrange the store so you can't find them. It's part of their marketing strategy. Maybe while you are looking you'll accidently buy something else you didn't realize you needed.

Let's say you find something at the Mall but decide to shop around, hoping to find the same item in another store for a lower price. It's now a few hours later, you've been through what seems like a hundred stores, and it's time to go back and get that item you wanted to buy. Only which store was it in, and will it still be there? Plus your shopping partner is tired and ready to go home. If you find the right store again, the salesperson you talked to before has gone home. The new salesperson vaguely remembers seeing something like what you want but can't quite put their finger on it. You know it was there earlier. What do you do?

Answer: the next time you find something you want at the Mall, just buy it. If you're smart, you'll buy two or three.

Parking your car at the airport can be an adventure as well. I once went on a business trip for two weeks, leaving my car in the parking garage at the Atlanta Airport. When I returned I discovered another car parked in the location where I had left my car. After dragging my luggage for 30 minutes all over both parking levels just to be sure, I went back into the terminal to contact the police. Surely my car had been stolen. At that point someone in the terminal mentioned a third parking level below the other two. Sure enough, there was my car right where I had left it on the third (bottom) level I didn't know existed.

I'm not saying that Y's don't ever encounter difficulty finding things. But when they do there is always an explanation. They ask their spouse, children, dog, roommate, etc. and someone confesses to moving the item of interest. Or they

Newton & Einstein, Stuff They Didn't Tell You

suddenly remember they moved it themselves when they were cleaning out the garage.

But for us N's there are no convenient explanations. In our case there is only one possibility. Mother Nature is to blame.

One more version of the Shell Game is when things come with identical parts that aren't (identical, that is). Examples of such things include:
- Round shaving heads in a rotary electric razor,
- Turbine blades in jet engines,
- Extra shirt buttons,
- Expensive tires for your sporty Nissan 350Z
- Ink cartridges for your computer printer,
- Twins that look alike but have different personalities (a fact you discover after you date both of them thinking it's the same girl).

Newton & Einstein, Stuff They Didn't Tell You

MG No. 2 – Aggravated Futility

This mind game employs the maximum expenditure of effort principle, using repetition to create a sense of futility.

You've experienced this if you can recall a situation where you had to run as hard as you could just to stay in the same place. The Greeks visualized futility as a man pushing a large stone ball almost to the top of a hill and then losing control, watching the ball roll back down to the bottom of the hill. The man (obviously an N) does this every day of his life (sound like anyone we know?).

Aggravated Futility usually happens when you are putting something together that has lots of parts.

Here are some examples:
- The last threaded socket in a long succession will be the one to foul up (cross thread, strip, break, etc.), making the entire assembly worthless (futility at its best).
- After completing the assembly and putting all the tools away you then find the gasket was left out (you got it together once, bet you can't do it again!).
- Your job is to write design specifications for a politically motivated $1,500,000,000 project the government never intends to actually build. Every design comment you resolve generates two new comments (but Congress keeps funding the work).
- You establish a four-year foreign policy goal to create a lasting peace between religious factions that have been at war for over 2000 years; when you're re-elected you establish a new foreign policy goal to do the same thing.

Some of Mother Nature's favorite (non-human) creatures play an active part in her Aggravated Futility schemes. Among these are fire ants, your neighbor's dog, and black birds. If you live in a southern state and have ever tried to get rid of fire ant mounds you understand the meaning of the word futility. Even those products that guarantee to kill the entire colony, including the queen, don't. The

Newton & Einstein, Stuff They Didn't Tell You

mounds you treat will die but others even larger will spring up across the lawn within a week. Keeping the number of mounds to less than ten per acre is about the best you can expect.

And you always find them when you're mowing the grass (another exercise in futility).

Equally daunting is keeping your neighbor's dog out of your flower beds. Dogs, especially your neighbor's, love the smell and feel of freshly turned soil. Your new azaleas just don't have a chance. Here again there are products on the market that guarantee to stop this sort of thing. I think my neighbor's dog actually gets "high" on this stuff. He keeps coming back for more. Then there are the blackbirds. These things apparently eat a certain kind of berry that turns to hydrochloric acid in their digestive tracts. The challenge is to wash your car and get it into the garage before the blackbirds spot it. If you are quick you can save the finish on your car. Those who leave the car out overnight suffer the consequences.

Did I mention that Mother Nature owns a garage where they repaint cars?

I've heard many say that working for the government is the ultimate act of futility, similar to riding a merry-go-round that never stops and doesn't have a brass ring. Some say it's because the government doesn't function very efficiently. Actually using the words "government" and "efficient" in the same sentence is an oxymoron all by itself. Aggravation comes to those who insistent upon trying to accomplish something. It's much easier if you just relax and enjoy the ride.

Working on government projects is like waking up with the same headache every day.

The people who run these projects often claim to have ten or more years of project management experience. Actually most of them just have one year's experience ten times in a row. That's because most government projects don't survive beyond the first year. They may go on and on for five or even ten years,

Newton & Einstein, Stuff They Didn't Tell You

but the real work gets done in the first twelve months. The rest of the time is devoted to revising, repackaging and resubmitting to Congress for more funding. Try comparing the number of projects the government has designed vs. the number that have actually been built and operated. I'm not claiming the government has a monopoly on Aggravated Futility. I just don't see any organization operating in the commercial sector even claiming to be in second place.

It is often said that our federal government would go bankrupt in two months or less if it had to compete fairly with commercial businesses. One reason may be that Mother Nature had a hand in designing most governmental procedures. You guessed it; they are all designed to achieve the ultimate in Aggravated Futility. To illustrate this point, it is worth noting that from a psychological perspective most government procedures are upside down. That is, they consistently penalize people for doing the right things and reward people for doing the wrong things.

Let's consider a few examples of how this works (or doesn't work):

- Careful and attentive managers who accomplish all of their work scope within budget can expect a reduced budget next year; those who pay little attention to spending rates and run out of money before year-end, can successfully argue for (and get) a larger budget next year. {Good management never goes unpunished.}
- Large contracts (e.g., $5 million) are often awarded to "sole source" contractors because someone already knows the "caliber of their work"; smaller contracts have to be posted on Commerce Business Daily, followed by a government "Request for Bids", formal Bid Submittals, evaluation by a Source Evaluation Board, etc. By the time the contract is actually awarded the government has spent up to half the money just picking the winning contractor. {Small efficient contractors can't compete with bigger less efficient ones.}
- People who are technical experts in their field can't change the "cost, scope or schedule" for government projects; only purchasing agents who aren't technically trained are allowed to make such changes. {Projects get

accepted as complete even though they are technically unacceptable}

- Broad "cookie-cutter" Plans are required for complex multi-year Projects; smaller short-term tasks require very detailed Plans that get stuck in the "review, comment and revise" cycle. {Eventually even the author forgets why the task was needed in the first place.}
- The more important a decision, the longer it takes to find someone who will make it. An often-used tool for delaying decisions is the National Environmental Protection Act (NEPA) process. {Decision avoidance is the key to success for career bureaucrats; they get promoted for avoiding decisions and punished for making them.}
- Making a decision is acceptable only when the decision-maker can demonstrate that they were overcome by events outside their control and therefore had no choice {Everyone can successfully deny responsibility}.
- Funding is distributed to government agencies based on Congressional handshakes, not on which government Projects are most important or would provide the greatest benefit for the money. {Politics trumps science and engineering every time.}
- Technical experts are encouraged to share their knowledge with peers and to document technical information, but find they are targets for downsizing (layoffs) if they do. {Technical experts must jealously hoard knowledge to secure their continued employment.}
- Government Project Managers enjoy greater job security than is available in the commercial sector:
    - They don't have to technically understand what they manage.
    - Government procedures require so many co-signatures on every document that no one can actually be held accountable (dilution of accountability).
    - They often continue to receive funding once the Project organization reaches "critical mass", even if the "mission" of the Project is delayed indefinitely.
    - They can move on to manage another government Project if their current Project fails or is cancelled without any stigma attached. {Incentives to efficiently manage Projects range from weak to nonexistent.}

Newton & Einstein, Stuff They Didn't Tell You

One more example of Aggravated Futility involves going in circles. Going in circles is Mother Nature's favorite form of motion because you are guaranteed to expend energy (and/or money) without making progress.

Said another way, progress is a vector not a scalar. One of my former engineering managers used to interrupt our project design meetings by commenting, "What we have here is activity masquerading as progress!" Regardless of how you state it, Mother Nature loves to put us in situations where we work hard only to find ourselves back where we started. Selling something for one price and buying that same item back later for a higher price is a perfect example of Aggravated Futility. I recall a number of times when Al Bundy did exactly that. Most N's have done it at least once.

It's worth noting that many government bureaucrats have built entire careers around the principle of Aggravated Futility.

Newton & Einstein, Stuff They Didn't Tell You

MG No. 3 – The Simplicity Con

Tasks that appear to be simple can become unbelievably complicated with a little help from Mother Nature; it's one of her favorite ways of tricking us N's into thinking we have enough time and energy to get something done.

Plumbing repairs are a good example.

If you purchase a 1940's vintage house you may find that all the water piping is screwed metal pipe. No problem as long as the builder took the trouble to install a coupling every so often so that you can take the system apart. Mother Nature helps you forget to ask such questions before all the mortgage papers are signed. Six months later you cut into the system to install a line for your washing machine. It's a simple job, right? It won't take more than an hour or two. Then you notice there are no couplings. The only way to finish what you've started is to go all the way back to the last joint and install a coupling. Except the hardware store doesn't carry couplings this size, so you also need a reducer on each end.

But now you also need a pipe threading machine. Even most Y's don't have one of these. The good news is you can rent one from the hardware store, just as soon as the guy who rented the last one this morning brings it back. I could keep going with this little story, but you'll notice a pattern here. Mother Nature has cleverly sucked you into a job that's getting more and more complicated by the moment. It's like quicksand. The more you try to escape the deeper you sink.

Of course the solution is to hire a professional plumber, who happens to mention all the plumbing problems the previous owner was having before he cleverly sold the place to you.

Changing the oil in the car is another job us N's usually feel qualified to perform. How difficult can it be? You take out the little plug at the bottom of the oil pan, let the oil drain out, and then put the plug back in. Refill the engine with new oil and you're all done. If it were only that simple. Remember the law of Irrational Resistance? Now the oil pan is a part of your car you don't want to have to

Newton & Einstein, Stuff They Didn't Tell You

replace. It's not a job we N's want to tackle. The little plug that unscrews from the bottom of the oil pan is easily replaced, at least in theory. The oil pan is not.

Given all this, what do you suspect the odds are that the little plug will cross thread when you try to put it back in? Buying a new plug is easy, so you know the male threads on the plug won't be damaged. No, it's the female threads on the oil pan that get stripped. Congratulations, you just saved $20 by changing your own oil, but it cost you $300 to get a new oil pan installed. Mother Nature does her best to stimulate the local economy when she can.

Look! The sign out front even says "Mother's Garage".

Other examples of the Simplicity Con include:
- Cleaning out the gutters (Hint: it's not the gutters, it's the ladders that get you in trouble),
- Painting your house (yep, it's those ladders again),
- Re-tiling a bathroom (rub the grout into your eyes, it will be less painful),
- Re-wallpapering (Hint: send the spouse to Hawaii for the week if you want to save money and your sanity),
- Changing the spark plugs on that old Chevrolet (remember the one where you couldn't get the last spark plug out without removing the engine?),
- Teaching your child to drive a car (Please leave this job to the professionals. We'll all feel safer, thank you!).

Newton & Einstein, Stuff They Didn't Tell You

Chapter Seven
Mind Games II

The beauty of Mother Nature's mind games is that she makes you believe it's all your fault. No special physical laws to blame this time. It's just your failing mental capacity, pure and simple. In the next mind game, the last shall be first and the first shall be last.

MG No. 4 – The Shortest Line Con

All of us have some experience standing in lines (or queues as they say in England) . The more crowded this planet becomes, the more we have to stand in line at the bank, grocery store, the pharmacy, etc. to get what we want. If you are (or were) in the military you know you have to stand in line for everything. In these situations it's only human nature to get into the line that looks the shortest.

Mother Nature takes great pleasure in reminding you that it was your choice, and making sure you regret it.

Back in the 1980's I visited a major discount store to purchase a few fishing lures. Naturally, I got in the shortest checkout line. The person in front of me had about a dozen items. When it became their turn they announced to the cashier that they wanted to split their items into two separate purchases. They wanted to pay for the first group of items partly with cash and partly using a gift certificate. And they wanted to pay for the second group of items partly with cash and partly with a credit card. In addition they had some discount coupons, but they weren't sure how to apply them to the two groups of items so as to get the greatest savings. I could tell by the look on the cashier's face that this was a "ten" on the "degree of difficulty" scale. To make a long story short (I know – too late) this person bought eleven items for a total of $38.23 in two transactions, which took a total of eighteen minutes.

Newton & Einstein, Stuff They Didn't Tell You

Now while I am standing there marveling at the complexity of this process, I couldn't help but notice how many checkout lanes were open and how long on average it took to let each customer pay for their merchandise. Here's the math. Four checkout lanes were operating. The average time to check out one customer was six minutes. That adds up to four customers every six minutes or forty customers per hour. Next, I estimated the average amount being spent by each customer at about $30.00. So now we have forty customers per hour times $30.00 per customer equals $1200.00 in gross sales per hour, or (based on a generous 20% profit margin) about $240.00 per hour in net revenue.

Next, I considered the employee payroll for a store this size.

Based on the number of people wearing the store logo on their shirts I estimated that about thirty people were getting paid to work in the store at that particular time. If these people were being paid an average of $7.00 per hour, then the payroll alone was $210.00 per hour (not including employer-paid Social Security tax, etc.). From all this I concluded that even if the only cost to run this store was the employee payroll (not very likely), at a rate of only four customers every six minutes that store could only turn a profit of $30.00 ($240.00 minus $210.00) per hour or maybe $360.00 per day. To this day I wonder how that could possibly be enough to keep senior management or the stockholders happy.

Even if the average customer bought twice as much as I assumed, it's still not nearly enough to keep the store in business.

So what's wrong with this picture?!

An average of six minutes to checkout one customer (or three times that long in my case) is not only frustrating for the customers, it also severely constrains the store's potential profits. Sales are further depressed when customers discover how long it takes to buy something at this store and choose to go elsewhere in the future (e.g., to find a shorter line). This example just shows that Mother Nature not only picks on individuals, she can screw up entire corporations if no one is "minding the store".

Newton & Einstein, Stuff They Didn't Tell You

Shortly after I moved to Alabama (also in the early 1980's) I went to the Alabama Highway Department to get new license plates for two cars and a pop-up camper. As soon as I walked into the building it was obvious that something was amiss. There were five lines of people waiting, four long ones and one with only three people in it. I looked for some clue to explain why one line was so much shorter. Finding nothing, I got in the short line. After about ten minutes I reached the counter. The lady behind the counter politely asked what type of farm vehicle I wanted to register. Farm vehicle?? When I told the lady that I wanted to register two cars and a camper-trailer she looked at me as though I had wasted her time. "You are in the wrong line", she said rather gruffly. I then asked how a person was supposed to know that this line was only for farm vehicles. "Oh", she said, "Everyone who lives here knows that".

With Mother Nature's help, the Alabama vehicle registration office had apparently decided that no one from outside the immediate neighborhood would ever need a car registration or license plate.

During a two-week visit in Europe in 2005 I noticed something about people waiting in lines. They often don't! It's not that they are impolite. It's just that the idea hasn't occurred to them that someone who has been waiting longer should be served sooner. You can tell the non-Europeans at ticket counters right away. They are the people looking around for the end of the line. It often takes them a while to realize there isn't one. I remember standing in line at an eyeglasses store, waiting for the next salesperson to become available. There were about six people standing (there were no chairs to sit in while you waited). A lady walked in, went straight to the counter and demanded to be served next. The salesperson behind the counter ignored her and took the next person in line. However, the next salesperson to step behind the counter waited on the lady who had just come in.

Mother Nature has a difficult time in Europe getting people to fall for her old shortest line gag. I believe I actually met one of her cousins in that European eyeglasses store.

Newton & Einstein, Stuff They Didn't Tell You

A variation of the "shortest line con" is the "faster moving line con". This is when you notice that people in another line seem to be moving more quickly than you are. The lady in the red dress is twelfth in her line and you are twelfth in yours. A moment later there are only eight people in front of her but there are still ten people in front of you. A few minutes later she is at the counter while you still have six people ahead of you. In fact everyone who came in about the time you did is now at the counter or has already completed their business and left.

Congratulations! The person handling your line just happens to be either a trainee or the slowest person on the face of the Earth.

Now here is where the "con" comes in. You feel stupid because with eight lines to pick from, you chose the one being handled by an elderly turtle. You are also frustrated because you had other errands to run, but now you won't have time. Stop beating yourself up. It didn't matter which of the eight lines you chose. Mother Nature simply waited to see which line you picked and then arranged for the turtle (who was returning from a forty-minute smoke break) to be there to greet you (eventually). Remember, whichever line you chose will always end up being the slowest. If you jump to the faster line, it will immediately slow down while the line you left will speed up.

It works the same way during highway construction delays. It's one of Mother Nature's little guarantees.

Newton & Einstein, Stuff They Didn't Tell You

MG No. 5 – Locational Amnesia

A good example of Locational Amnesia is when you get up from the sofa and go into another room to get something, except that when you get there you can't remember what you came to get. You can stand there until you have a mental hernia. It's no use. You will only remember when you go back to your original location.

As soon as your rear end touches the sofa again, it all comes back to you.

Another example of Locational Amnesia involves parties, grocery stores and other public places where you are likely to run into old acquaintances you haven't seen for a while. You know the drill. Someone walks up to you, pats you on the back and asks how you've been. You want to introduce him to your fiancée but you haven't a clue who he is. You listen intently for a tip in the conversation, but it's no help. Finally, in desperation you ask him to remind you how he spells his name so you can send him a Christmas card.

Looking puzzled, he spells his name for you: B-R-O-W-N.

And when you go to the grocery store or pharmacy, why can't you remember the five items you came to buy? You didn't bother to make a list before you left home. There were only five items; how could you possibly forget just five items? By not making the list you set yourself up for Mother Nature to distract you with that friend you don't remember or some other event. And the most fun for her is when you blame yourself. After all, it's your fault you didn't make the list. If you had, that distraction wouldn't have mattered (and Mother Nature wouldn't have bothered to arrange it in the first place).

Sometimes we confuse Locational Amnesia and the Shell Game. Mother Nature doesn't care what you call it. It's just as much fun for her either way.

Take your car keys for example. You come in from the store, toss your car keys down, and start putting away the groceries. Then the phone rings, the kids come

Newton & Einstein, Stuff They Didn't Tell You

in from school, etc. An hour later you're ready to go out again. Where are the car keys? You know you threw them down somewhere, but where? Has Mother Nature deceived you into thinking you threw them on the kitchen table, when you didn't? Do you have to be in the same room with them before you'll remember?

So you retrace your steps back to when you came in with the groceries. Still no success. Finally, one of the kids walks in the room holding your keys, asking "Is this what you're looking for? I found them on top of the television". You can't remember going anywhere near the television all day.

Most of us associate certain locations with a specific daily routine. If you have a security badge you know that arriving at work without it means a trip back home to get it and late arrival at the office. If you happen to have an early meeting that day then you also have to confess your sins to a group of strangers. Therefore, to make certain you never forget your security badge you construct a foolproof routine. It involves the dresser in your bedroom where you carefully place your badge the instant you arrive home each day from work. No matter what's going on when you get home, you know you have to put your security badge on the dresser in the bedroom before you do anything else.

The bad part about daily routines is that 1) you count on them to work, and 2) when they don't work you're completely lost.

One morning you wake up, shower, get dressed, eat breakfast and reach for your security badge on the dresser in the bedroom. Like a lightning bolt it hits you. Your badge is gone! An immediate feeling of complete hopelessness sweeps over you. You haven't got a clue. You don't even know where to start looking. Mother Nature knows where your badge is and she isn't going to tell you until one hour later when it shows up in the seat of your car. "How did it get there", you ask?

Like any good magician, Mother Nature never reveals how her tricks are done.

Newton & Einstein, Stuff They Didn't Tell You

Other locations that have the ability to wipe your memory banks clean include:
- Your supervisor's office, especially when the FBI is present,
- Divorce court (yours),
- Shopping Mall parking lots (they all look the same)
- Center stage in front of a large audience,
- In front of CNN News Cameras (they're live, you wish you weren't)
- Your child's bedroom when they ask you to explain about sex.

Newton & Einstein, Stuff They Didn't Tell You

MG No. 6 – Invisible Mistakes

Have you ever noticed that it's practically impossible to find your own mistakes?

If you make an error in computing your taxes, it will be invisible to you, but the tax auditor will spot it in less than five minutes. When you write a report even your computer spell checker doesn't notice that you typed the word "two" when you meant "too". But your boss will spot the misspelling as soon as he turns the page. If you are an N Mother Nature has a nasty habit of embedding subtle mistakes in your work, and she does it in a manner that makes them impossible for you to find.

Of course all mistakes are invisible until someone finds them. Most are found before they do any real harm. Others, especially the ones that make the headlines, don't get found until it's too late. And then there are those mistakes that don't appear to be mistakes until something unexpected happens.

Consider a mistake that made headlines around the world, the nuclear reactor accident at Chernobyl in 1986.

RBMK reactors like the one at Chernobyl were designed so that portions of the reactor could be shipped in sections that were compatible with the limited transportation available in portions of the Former Soviet Union (FSU). Without explaining all the physics involved, this design resulted in what is known as a "reactor with positive void coefficients". In layman's terms this means that if the water that removes heat from the reactor begins to boil, steam bubbles will make the nuclear reaction accelerate. This is analogous to having your car suddenly begin to accelerate on its own if you push the gas pedal past a certain point. To make matters worse, a nuclear reactor doesn't have an ignition key you can just switch off. Reactors in the United States and most other countries are designed with negative void coefficients, meaning if the coolant boils the nuclear reaction will slow down or stop altogether.

Newton & Einstein, Stuff They Didn't Tell You

To most nuclear engineers, the design of the RBMK reactor at Chernobyl was a mistake, an accident waiting to happen. Events that took place in the reactor building during the hours just prior to the fire and meltdown of the reactor have been analyzed many times and are often blamed for the accident, but the real culprit was an unsafe design. And yet to those who developed the RBMK design it was the only feasible way to bring electrical power to a region of the Former Soviet Union that badly needed it.

To them it was not a mistake at all, until it was too late.

Mistakes can be also be hidden from us. A common piece of advice for someone about to purchase a new car is, "Don't buy a car assembled on Monday morning or Friday afternoon". The thought behind this is that on Monday morning people make more mistakes because they are still thinking about the weekend past. And on Friday afternoon people make more mistakes because their minds are on the coming weekend. Even if this wisdom isn't accurate most of the time, why take the chance?

I've also found, sadly, that there are automobile dealerships that like working on your car a little too much. It seems that every time they fix one problem, they find a subtle way of creating another that brings you back a few weeks later. I first suspected Mother Nature was playing one of her pranks, but the evidence pointed to someone human. An ordinary oil change led to a failed water pump bearing (they over tightened the belt), followed by a failed water hose (it was cleverly cut), followed by a failed headlight (pinhole made by the point of a screwdriver), followed by my certified letter to the Manager of the Dealership and the Regional Manager.

I sold that car six months later and have never owned that make of car since.

There are some mistakes we make deliberately just to see if anyone will notice.

I recall a young engineer who held a rather low opinion of his management. In fact he was convinced that none of his supervisors ever read his documents even

Newton & Einstein, Stuff They Didn't Tell You

though they authorized them for publication. One day he decided to add a little something to one of his routine monthly reports, betting that no one would notice. In the middle of page seventeen of a twenty-four page report he inserted the words "Jack screwed Jill up on the Hill, forget the pail of water". Maybe his manager's weren't paying attention, but Mother Nature was. His report made it through the first three levels of management, but the Vice President decided to pick one monthly report out of the stack and read it. Guess which one he picked.

Miraculously, the young engineer's career survived. Two of his supervisor's didn't.

One final category of Invisible Mistakes is worth special consideration. Have you ever wondered how many of your mistakes never revealed themselves? You didn't notice them, no one else ever pointed them out to you, and as far as you know nothing bad resulted from them. Certainly some of your mistakes have never been discovered (like transposing the last two digits on your mortgage interest deduction in 1999). They remain invisible to this day. How could Mother Nature let you get away with that? Actually, the question is "How long will Mother Nature let you get away with that?" And when will she decide to reveal your hidden mistake?

Answer: Whenever you least expect it!

How about those mistakes you might have made but didn't. What if life is like a giant computer code, written to cover all the foreseeable paths your life can take. Then some parts of that computer code will never get used. For example the program intended to cover your career as a brain surgeon never got activated because you decided to be an engineer instead. There may be any number of mistakes you were supposed to make as a brain surgeon, but they never happened. Likewise the mistakes you were supposed to make during your vacation in Michigan. Except you went to Hawaii that year, and have never been to Michigan.

You also didn't get married, which accounts for quite a few.

Newton & Einstein, Stuff They Didn't Tell You

Now it's time to add up the score on mistakes. Why bother with the Y's. Let's just say you're an N.

By the time you are in your early sixty's you will have probably made a total of 3159 mistakes:
- 251 of these were discovered by you,
- 1937 were discovered by others,
- 971 are waiting to be discovered (at Mother Nature's discretion),
- 1140 have been forgiven,
- 98 had serious consequences,
- 19 permanently scarred your life or someone else's,
- 16 you would give anything if you could undo, and
- 7 that actually turned out for the best (i.e., Mother Nature wasn't paying attention and you got away with these).

And, lest we not forget, you were supposed to make a grand total of 25,967 mistakes, but only if you had been a brain surgeon, corporate CEO, stock broker, lawyer, automobile mechanic, and lobster fisherman all in the same lifetime.

I'd say you've done pretty well.

Newton & Einstein, Stuff They Didn't Tell You

Chapter Eight
Mind Games III

Some of Mother Nature's mind games are very subtle. It's like watching a magician doing those slight of hand or misdirection tricks. She counts on you looking at one hand while she's slipping it to you with the other. But just try to catch her at it.

MG No. 7 – The "Set-up"

This is one of Mother Nature's most insidious pranks because you only recognize it after it happens, and what's worse, you did it to yourself.

The set-up is where you take extra precautions to prevent disaster, only to find that the disaster still occurs and those extra precautions you took have mysteriously conspired to amplify the consequences. The simplest example is when your spouse asks if the dress she's wearing makes her look fat. You know you have to be very careful with your answer, but hesitation will get you into trouble as well. So you say "Dear, nothing in your closet makes you look slimmer than that dress".

One hour later you're at the Mall with your spouse picking out her new wardrobe.

For a less expensive example, let's take cooking. You've carefully chopped up some spices ahead of time and put them in a bowl. Being an N, you know that if you set the bowl next to where you are working Mother Nature will find some way to make you knock it over spilling your spices onto the floor. So you carefully plan a way to prevent this from happening. You place the bowl on a shelf in the refrigerator where it will be safely out of your way. You then

Newton & Einstein, Stuff They Didn't Tell You

proceed; confident you have foiled at least one of Mother Nature's plans to ruin your day.

A few minutes later you discover the recipe calls for mayonnaise. You take the mayonnaise jar from the refrigerator, spoon out the correct amount and put the jar back into the refrigerator. Now you are almost done. All you need are those spices you prepared earlier. You reach into the refrigerator, proudly retrieving the bowl that Mother Nature couldn't make you spill; and this is when she gets you. The law of Mischievous Attraction makes the jar of mayonnaise come with it.

Onto the floor it goes.

Now, instead of a pile of dry spices to clean up you have almost a full quart of greasy mayonnaise mixed with broken glass on the floor. That is when it hits you. It wasn't the spices Mother Nature was going for. It was the mayonnaise all along. In this example the principle of Maximum Effort ensures that more time will be spent cleaning up the mayonnaise and broken glass than you were going to spend cooking your dinner in the first place. Also, since you were at the last step of preparing that dinner you can add all that wasted effort as well.

Final score: Two hours wasted and no dinner to show for it.

What makes the set-up so much fun for Mother Nature is that she uses your own resourcefulness against you. If you hadn't put the bowl of spices in the refrigerator, the worst that could have happened was spilling a few spices. You could have cleaned that up and chopped more spices in a fraction of the time it took to clean up the mayonnaise and broken glass. By trying to outwit her you unknowingly amplified the consequences ten-fold. Some N's I know have given up entirely on the notion that they can ever outwit Mother Nature. They would rather just take what she dishes out instead of making it ten times worse.

Both mechanical and electronic devices offer Mother Nature the opportunity to add insult to injury. As you are probably aware, most of these devices are

Newton & Einstein, Stuff They Didn't Tell You

designed so that the parts that fail are relatively inaccessible. The manufacturer doesn't want you to fix it yourself. They just want to sell you a new one.

In fact some devices contain one or more parts that have been engineered with a programmed life expectancy. That helps the manufacturers accurately predict replacement sales.

Being the victim of a manufacturer's planned failure rate is normal for both Y's and N's. But when N's try to make repairs rather than pay full price for a replacement, it's the perfect set-up. Even though the part that fails is supposedly inaccessible, you know that all you have to do is take off a few other parts that are in the way. How hard can that be? So you remove these other parts, laying them carefully aside in an organized manner, remembering how to put them back again. Then you remove the failed part, buy a replacement for a small fraction of the cost of an entire new machine, and reinstall.

Now the fun begins.

One or more of those good parts you took off to get to the failed part won't go back on. Either you break it trying to reinstall it or you can't reinstall it at all. In the end you spend a lot of money for replacement parts that weren't originally broken, or you give up and go buy a whole new machine, which is what the manufacturer wanted you to do in the first place. This is when you notice an access panel on the other side, designed to allow you to get to the part that originally failed without removing anything else. Of course, you're an N and would have never suspected the manufacturer (or Mother Nature) would make the job that easy.

Mother Nature can also persuade your favorite pet to turn on you when you least expect it.

It may be something simple like that television commercial that shows the dog putting his paw on the button that locks the man out of his car. How can you blame the dog in this case? He didn't know what he was doing, or did he?

Newton & Einstein, Stuff They Didn't Tell You

Mother Nature takes full advantage of the fact that you love your pet and would never believe that it could do something malicious on purpose.

Here are some other things your favorite pet probably does that you routinely forgive them for:
- Wets the carpet just before company arrives,
- Chews the newspaper until it's unreadable,
- Sharpens their claws on the upholstered furniture,
- Uses your new silk blouse as a wrestle-toy ,
- Leaves "presents" in your favorite slippers,
- Refuses to eat until you guess which flavor of cat food it wants today,
- Leaves muddy footprints on your freshly washed car
- Drags their "catch of the day" into your living room while you are serving cheese and crackers to your guests.

Remember, this is an animal you can't train to do anything, yet it somehow chooses just the right time to embarrass you in front of your friends. Timing is everything, but I'll have more to say about that in Chapter Fifteen.

Never underestimate Mother Nature's influence over animals. She knows they can't testify against her.

Newton & Einstein, Stuff They Didn't Tell You

MG No. 8 – Visual Blitzkrieg

One more example of Mischievous Attraction is the irresistible bond Mother Nature creates between people and television sets. Invisible shackles hold people in a state of semi-conscious addiction, even when there is nothing on TV worth watching. Either that, or people spend hours in front of the TV simply because they have nothing better to do with their time. I refuse to believe that explanation.

People who write television commercials are well aware of Mother Nature's power to hypnotize the masses. For almost fifty years they have conspired to use that power to make people buy stuff. Remember, without Mother Nature's influence there would be far fewer television commercials because people would simply get up and go do something productive every time a commercial came on. The fact that they don't is hard evidence of a conspiracy.

The ability to digitize images has allowed television advertisers to reach new highs.

For example, "important messages" are now brought to you by talking animals. These range from gecko's with British accents to indignant Chihuahuas to happy California cows. Are talking animals more credible than humans? If so, why? Do we trust a talking chicken more than those attractive people on CNN?

Some TV commercials deliberately flash images at you so rapidly that your brain can't catch up. Mother Nature must have called Madison Avenue and pointed out the fact that, given time to look at an image, people can readily dismiss stuff that looks unbelievable. In other words, they just don't buy it, literally. But if you flash images at people so quickly that they never get a good look, some folks may come away with a subliminal urge to go buy something they have no use for.

And that's what it's all about. You already have everything you need. It's time to sell you all that other stuff no sane person would purchase.

Newton & Einstein, Stuff They Didn't Tell You

In America cable and satellite TV companies boast their ability to provide almost three-hundred channels of entertainment, even though it only takes about a week before you realize that two-hundred of these channels never show anything you are even remotely interested in, and another fifty show the same stuff over and over again month after month. That leaves you with about fifty channels that are worth surfing when you're tired of that program you're currently watching. Fortunately channel surfing has been simplified to the point of being almost effortless. By pushing only two or three buttons you can read a summary of what's on each and every channel, when it starts, who's starring in it, etc.

If you want to actually watch a channel you just push one more button, unless the program on that channel is scheduled to be completed in less than ten minutes. You see Mother Nature designed your "surfable" menu on some TVs so that it automatically changes at ten minutes before the hour and ten minutes before the half-hour to show what's coming on ten minutes from now, not what's on now. If you want to know what's on now you have to make the menu go back half an hour. You can also take the menu forward to show what will be on two hours from now or even tomorrow.

Sometimes the complexity of manipulating the channel menu can be more entertaining than actually finding a program to watch.

Eventually you will grow tired of just surfing the channel menu and actually select a channel to watch (if you happen to be within that twenty minute window when the menu shows what is actually on). At this point another tell-tale sign of Mother Nature's handiwork becomes evident. Any channel you select will be showing a TV commercial at that moment, not the movie or program you wanted to watch. It doesn't matter when you chose to surf the menu. The result is always the same. You will get an advertisement for car insurance, fast food, floor cleaner, etc.

If you happen to be really lucky you may tune in just at the beginning of an eclectic string of ads that have nothing to do with one another but seem to go on forever. If you happen to be near the end of a particularly suspenseful movie

Newton & Einstein, Stuff They Didn't Tell You

there can be up to fifteen thirty-second ads all strung together like Christmas tree ornaments collected by fifteen different families. Showing exactly the same ad twice in a row (just to get you to notice) is particularly annoying.

Companies that chose that advertising technique can rest assured that I wouldn't purchase their product if it was water and I was dying of thirst.

But let's get back to that stuff you don't need.

What are people willing to pay for stuff they don't need. Mother Nature has the answer. She knows your financial "threshold of concern". It turns out that the average person's "threshold of concern" is about $20.00. Most of us are willing to lose that much in a Friday night poker game without being bothered too much. In fact, if you're an N you pretty much write off that $20.00 when you sit down at the table. So if you are trying to use television to sell people stuff they don't need, where do you set the price? The obvious answer is $19.95 (not counting shipping and handling). If you price your unneeded product higher than that some people will notice that it's more than $20.00 and get concerned about whether they really need this thing you're selling. On the other hand, if you price your product well below $20.00 then people will think it's junk and they have enough junk already.

As you can see, $19.95 is like Baby Bear's porridge. It is not too hot and not too cold. It's just right.

Have you ever sat watching an American football game on TV when the cameramen lost track of where the ball was and missed the play? Did you think to yourself "How could I have been fooled into watching that running back when it was a pass play all along"? Then it dawns on you (I hope) that you weren't fooled at all. You were stuck with wherever the cameraman happened to be pointing his camera. You just took the blame for something you didn't even do!

Another mindset we can thank advertisers and Mother Nature for is this obsession with "New".

Newton & Einstein, Stuff They Didn't Tell You

If you want to sell a product it has to be "New", or at least a part of it has to be "New", or it has to be in a "New" package with a new name (so I can't find it anymore). I call this the "New" obsession: If it isn't "New", people won't buy it. But how can everything be new continuously? By definition, the label of "New" is perishable. New shopping centers are constructed to lure in more customers. But what about the old shopping centers, you know the ones that were "New" last year? Sadly most are abandoned in place for the community to dispose of.

If you're looking a tangible legacy from Mother Nature, abandoned stores and shopping centers are it.

Advertising executives have come to the conclusion that the words "new" and "exciting" are synonymous. You see it in their TV commercials and magazine ads constantly; every product is described as "new and exciting".

I think this is another of Mother Nature's slams on old people (see Chapter 19).

Logically, if "new" means "exciting", then "old" must mean "unexciting", dull, lifeless, etc. Most TV commercials and magazine ads show young people with fabulous bodies doing things most of us over sixty can only vaguely remember (if it was legal when we were twenty). How does it make us feel to know we aren't welcome on South Beach, Florida? Obviously, those advertising companies only consider the over-sixty crowd as consumers for laxatives, hemorrhoid creams, and retirement investment plans. I also know that old people go to Las Vegas. I know because I've been there and seen them blowing their life savings. But all the ads for Las Vegas are aimed at young people who don't yet have a life savings to blow.

You Ad Exec's need to wise up!

Newton & Einstein, Stuff They Didn't Tell You

MG No. 9 – Concealed Irreversibility

Everyone knows that once an egg is scrambled it can't be unscrambled. Many events are universally recognized as irreversible. You can't take them back to the original state no matter how hard you try. On the other hand many other events are commonly recognized as reversible. Things can be returned to the way they were, given enough time and energy, at least in theory.

Actually there is a third situation between the extremes of reversibility and irreversibility. It exists when an event appears to be reversible, but you find out too late that it isn't. The Pitcher Plant is an excellent example.

The Pitcher Plant is a carnivorous plant that has a slender vessel shape open at the top and contains sweet smelling nectar that attracts insects like bees and flies. When the insect lands at the plant's opening and begins to crawl down inside for the nectar, it fails to notice thousands of hairs that point downward toward the bottom of the vessel. Eventually the insect discovers that it can crawl down but never up. The insect dies and is consumed by the Pitcher Plant, a victim of concealed irreversibility. N's often find that Mother Nature has trapped them, at least temporarily, like the insect in the Pitcher Plant.

America's Interstate Highway system is good example. If a Y accidentally takes the wrong exit off an Interstate Highway, they simply wait for the traffic light to change, cross through the intersection and take the opposing entrance ramp to get back on. However, some exits are designed just for us N's. One of these is on Interstate 20 between Atlanta, Georgia and Augusta. Getting off at that exit guarantees the driver a scenic tour of the local town with all its traffic signals, and surrounding countryside to the east for about five miles of two-lane road. By the time you get back to Interstate 20, you've wasted about 20 minutes. What appears to be reversible (exit from an Interstate Highway) isn't.

In her usual style, Mother Nature arranges it so Y's never take that exit or others like it. She manages to warn the Y's but not the N's.

Newton & Einstein, Stuff They Didn't Tell You

I learned my first lesson in Concealed Irreversibility when I was 8 years old. I discovered with great surprise that the inside of my father's wind-up alarm clock was full of gears and other parts that moved in perfect unison, all apparently powered by a mainspring. And that mainspring, once removed, can't be rewound and put back on, no matter how hard you try. I was quite confused by this. Someone had to have assembled this clock from its pieces. One of those pieces was the mainspring. Therefore there must be a way to reverse my action of removing the mainspring from the clock. My next two week's allowance went to buy a new alarm clock. Since clocks these days don't have mainsprings, I suspect I will die never knowing how those old clocks got their mainsprings.

Did Mother Nature warn the Y's who were my age not to take apart alarm clocks? I still think she did.

Mother Nature adores "check valves" and "interlocks". A check valve is an engineered device that only lets stuff flow through a pipe in one direction. If the pressure in the pipe reverses, the check valve closes to prevent stuff from flowing back where it came from. This would be useful, for example, if you wanted to connect your drinking water piping to the city sewer system. You wouldn't want sewage to flow back up your drinking water line, would you? Fortunately some guy who fully understood the power of Mother Nature to circumvent any engineered device declared it illegal to connect drinking water piping to a sewer system, no matter how many check valves are used. However, there are still a great many engineered systems that rely on check valves. Interlocks are similar to check valves except that interlocks won't let stuff flow in either direction unless certain conditions are met, usually a complex combination of electrical signals, etc.

From time to time us N's have to repair things that have check valves and/or interlocks. Mother Nature makes sure we don't know the check valve or interlock is there. This can be great fun indeed.

Let's say your riding lawnmower won't start and you suspect it's because the fuel

Newton & Einstein, Stuff They Didn't Tell You

line is plugged. You try blowing into the engine's fuel line to remove whatever is plugging it. Blow as hard as you want. The line stays plugged, or so you think. So you buy a new section of fuel line and install it. The new line now acts like it's plugged as well. OK, it must be in the carburetor. After taking the carburetor apart you discover no problem on that end either. One week later the repair shop calls to say that your mower is fixed. It wasn't the fuel system at all, but something electrical instead. After the mechanic adds up your bill he casually mentions the check valve in the fuel system you didn't know was there.

You can hear him (and Mother Nature) laughing at you as you hang up the phone.

Occasionally Mother Nature finds a way to make things irreversible in both directions, like the movie about the guy living in the airport whose passport was revoked so that he couldn't fly on to his destination and he couldn't fly back home either. Do you think maybe this guy was an N? I remember my father telling me that he walked in three feet of snow to and from school each day and the trip was up hill both ways.

As an N I'm willing to consider the possibility that he wasn't exaggerating. Maybe Mother Nature found a way.

We've all heard of these plastic raincoats that come in tiny packages. It really is impossible to fold them small enough to fit back in that little bag they came in. I used to have an inflatable kayak that has a similar problem. It came in a canvas bag from the manufacturer with clear instructions on how to fold it back up so it would fit into the bag. After numerous tries I finally gave up and bought a new larger bag to keep it in.

Mother Nature can also be creative.

Take those pasteboard boxes that doughnuts come in. They are made to lay flat until the people at the doughnut shop fold them into the familiar box shape. Once they become boxes the same little flaps that laid flat before now stick out and prevent you from closing the box. Why should doughnut boxes be easy to open

Newton & Einstein, Stuff They Didn't Tell You

but hard to re-close? One side of the top will close but the other side of the top will catch on that side of the bottom. Then you get that side to close and the other side will catch on itself. Why should it take two hands to close a doughnut box when it only took one hand to open it? And the irony is that you had two free hands when you opened the box, but only one free hand (the other hand is holding your doughnut) when you want to close it.

See how creative Mother Nature can be!

Y's can take an umbrella that has been blown inside out and return it to its original shape without breaking it. N's just can't do that. If a circuit breaker in your house overloads and trips, get a Y to flip it back on. N's usually find the breaker won't reset and you're forced to install a new one. Reversible jackets aren't. And male N's know that zippers will often zip down but not back up, especially if you are in a public restroom. In fact Mother Nature loves to inflict clothing malfunctions in public places. For her it's a "no-brainer". If you've changed the water filter in your house, you know that the little o-ring seal won't (seal, that is) until you've taken it apart and put it back together at least three times. Mother Nature loves to make the o-ring pop out of its groove just as you are screwing the whole thing back together again.

Here are some other things that are supposed to be reversible, but may not be if you are an N:
- Identity Theft
- Publication of your email address
- Dissemination of your phone number to telemarketers
- Errors in your Credit Report
- Standing invitation to your mother-in-law to come for a visit
- Athlete's foot – Toe Nail Fungus
- Wedding Vows

Newton & Einstein, Stuff They Didn't Tell You

Chapter Nine
Maintaining Your Sanity

A question that sometimes drives me hazy: am I or are the others crazy?" - Albert Einstein

If you are a Type N person there are several things you can do to maintain your sanity. I mentioned one of these earlier. N's like to talk to themselves because verbalizing their predicament out loud releases some of the stress and frustration that's building up inside of them. It's like a pressure relief valve that absolutely must open occasionally to prevent the entire vessel from exploding.

When you hear an N talking (sometimes shouting), they are only angry with themselves (and Mother Nature), not with anyone else. Talking also helps to convince them that it's really happening.

It isn't just a bad dream. Mother Nature really is beating the crap out of them at that moment.

Of course venting your frustrations out loud can be distressing to your spouse or significant other, especially if they are a Y. So let's talk about relationships for a second.

Those Y – Y relationships don't require much discussion. Both of these people see life as reasonably benign. Mother Nature leaves them both alone so they only have each other to deal with. If they have occasional disagreements the matter can be settled by talking things out. Their life together is logical and explainable. N – N relationships can be reasonably benign as well. Mother Nature molests both parties on a regular basis. Both have similarly low expectations for

Newton & Einstein, Stuff They Didn't Tell You

individual success, but together they stand a better chance of getting what they want than they would separately. And each understands and sympathizes with the other when Mother Nature has dealt them a particularly bad day. Even when they both have a bad day they can sometimes find humor by sharing their stories.

What's left are the Y – N relationships.

Like Hollandaise sauce, these take constant attention to prepare and not much to make things separate. One person sees life as logical, predictable and "under control". The other sees life as too full of variables to be any of these things. Y's like to make decisions and execute them. N's like to plan alternatives and be prepared for the unexpected. N's talk to themselves out loud when things don't go well. Y's have no need to do this, and don't understand why their partner does. When a Y sees an N having difficulty, their response is to take over the task and complete it without incident. This leaves the N with a sense of incompetence and failure.

An N wants the chance to struggle with Mother Nature, not just have a Y come save them by hitting Mother Nature over the head with a frying pan. In summary, Y – N relationships can be difficult because there are three parties involved, and the third party is invisible to the Y. If you are an N, the easiest way to keep your sanity is to find another N to be happy with.

Of course if the love of your life turns out to be a Y then you have to find ways to cope. Believe it or not there are quite a few. But that's another book.

What about business relationships? Can a Y and an N work together? Yes, I've observed numerous examples of Y's and N's working together in harmony. The key to this arrangement is for the N's to recognize (privately and publicly) that the Y's are almost always right. Once this is established, things can move along quite well. In fact, with the Y's deciding and executing and the N's planning alternatives and expecting the unexpected some really great teamwork can occur. It took me several years to understand that all the hype about "diversity" in the workplace went beyond gender, race and ethnic background. It's all about Y's

Newton & Einstein, Stuff They Didn't Tell You

and N's teaming to develop omnipotent designs that neither could have produced by themselves.

N's sometimes find themselves in management positions with both N's and Y's reporting to them. If you've ever been the N in this situation you know that the issue here is getting the Y's to take you seriously. One way to deal with this is to actively involve your people (Y's and N's) in the decision making process. The Y's will claim credit for most of the good ideas and actively support their implementation. The N's will follow along developing alternatives and fallback positions because they can do that very well. You can then report the organization's success to your boss, proving your worth as good manager. If he also happens to be an N, your obvious skill at managing all those Y's will appear even more impressive.

While we're on the subject of management, let's look at what N's and Y's are best suited for.

Over the years I've worked for some very smart managers. One of them once reminded me that "You manage programs or assets, but you lead people". For example, you manage a project schedule, a budget, a safety program, a chain of hotels or a fleet of vehicles. Most people, however, resent being managed. They prefer to be lead. You lead a team of nuclear safety experts in an investigation of an accident. You lead a group of people developing a written bid proposal for a government contract. Leadership requires that you paint a vision of success, help people to collectively see that vision, and then inspire them to make it a reality during a finite time period.

You may have guessed that Y's make better leaders, and N's make better managers.

Well, you guessed wrong. Both Y's and N's make good managers and good leaders. They simply approach these jobs differently. Obviously, N's have to allow for Mother Nature's interference and Y's don't. Beyond that it's a matter of consistently making the best choices given the options that are available. Y's and

Newton & Einstein, Stuff They Didn't Tell You

N's do this differently but they both get it done. That's what counts to the people you lead and the customers you serve.

There should be a Web page designed specifically for N's. And it should not be accessible to Y's (so its content doesn't become the favorite topic at cocktail parties). This can easily be accomplished by requiring anyone attempting to access the Web site to log-on five times. The first four log-on attempts will link to porn sites selected at random. Y's (who are accustomed to getting what they want on the first or second try) will be discouraged or distracted (or both) and give up. Only N's (who consider success in less than five tries to be a miracle) will reach the Web site designed for them.

A Web site designed for N's should contain information that will help N's in their lifelong struggle with Mother Nature. Such a site might include:
- Tips for surviving Y – N relationships,
- Chat room for Toppers ("If you think that was bad, listen to what happened to me ...."),
- Code Breakers (tips for understanding why electronics don't work, plus a buyer's guide for N's),
- Fashion advice (what N's shouldn't wear in public),
- Photo gallery (notable examples of Mother Nature's cruel tricks caught on film or video),
- Clever comebacks you can use if you have to attend one of those Y dominated cocktail parties,
- Job search (employment opportunities for N's, posted by N's so you know they are for real),
- "Ain't it Awful" Contest (The ten most bizarre life stories posted each week with a way to vote for your favorite).

If anyone out there wants to create such a Web site, I say go for it!

Choosing the right place to live can also help us N's stay sane. You might think that N's should stay away from earthquake zones like California, tornado alley states like Nebraska, Kansas and Oklahoma, and especially southern Florida during hurricane season. Actually there's no need to take such precautions. As I

Newton & Einstein, Stuff They Didn't Tell You

mentioned earlier, Mother Nature doesn't get involved in causing illness, pain and death. Whatever made God mad at southern Florida during the 2004 hurricane season and the Gulf Coast in general during the 2005 hurricane season, it wasn't Mother Nature's doing. Us N's can feel as safe (or unsafe) as anyone else living in these locations.

If you're an N, choosing the right place to live means picking the right neighborhood. If you can find a subdivision or apartment complex where other N's tend to congregate, you'll have fewer Y's to envy. There will be more yards that have crabgrass like yours. You will be more likely to find other people who think your life story is not so unusual (and pathetic). Your neighbors won't call the police when they hear you shouting at the lawnmower. You may find a Friday night poker game or local bridge club that you can actually enjoy (see Chapter Twelve).

Maybe some folks will even get together and watch reruns of "Married with Children" and the Pink Panther movies.

There was a time when only Y's drove imported cars. That's because repair parts for these machines used to be hard to get, making them bad decisions for us N's. Parts for foreign cars are now stocked in U. S. warehouses. Now we N's can enjoy the luxuries of Japanese and European imports just like the Y's. If you want to preserve your sanity there is just one thing about imported cars you need to remember. They attract speeding tickets. Most people (Y's and N's) have suspected for some time that Highway Patrol Units use a quota system, i.e., each patrol squad must give out some minimum number of speeding tickets each month. If a squad doesn't meet their quota one month they are obviously not doing their job.

What isn't generally known is that many such quota systems use a graded approach.

It all goes back to the days when there weren't very many foreign cars on American highways. The graded approach awards points to the patrol squad for each speeding ticket based on the type of car that was speeding. American cars

Newton & Einstein, Stuff They Didn't Tell You

are worth one point each. Japanese cars are worth five points each. European cars are worth from eight to twenty points, depending on the make. Lamborghini's and Ferraris are worth forty-five points each, because there are relatively few of these in America, and the Highway Patrol cars usually can't catch them. So if you drive an imported car the Highway Patrol is hoping to catch you speeding. It's all about the points. Given that the cops are already looking for you and given that Mother Nature is helping them because you are an N, driving a foreign car is like wearing a big bull's-eye.

For an N sanity means driving an American car at or below the posted speed limit. (Y's can drive up to seven mph over the posted speed limit). If you must drive an import, make it Japanese. It makes the bull's-eye a little smaller.

While we are on the subject of cars and driving, it's time to discuss one of Mother Nature's favorite ways of entertaining herself. That would be fanning the flames of highway frustration, commonly known as "road rage". She does this in much the same way that Jerry Springer gets the "guests" (mostly N's) on his TV show to fight each other.

Have you noticed that some drivers like to stay in the inside lane on the Interstate regardless of their speed? Apparently they believe the inside lane is reserved just for the Y's of the world and the outside lane is for everyone else. Highway engineers responsible for designing our Interstate Highway system had a different idea in mind. Slower moving vehicles wouldn't have to make everyone slow down if the inside lane was always open so faster vehicles could to go around. In fact most four-lane highways have signs saying "Slower Traffic Keep Right".

Of course those "inside-laners" assume these signs don't apply to them. Mother Nature loves it when a "inside-laner" pulls up next to a truck or other slower vehicle in the outside lane and then proceeds to match speeds with them, trapping thirty or forty cars behind for the next twenty miles. It's hard to find another situation that can generate as much pure road rage and risky driving as this one. And the beauty of all this is that the "inside-laner" causing the problem

Newton & Einstein, Stuff They Didn't Tell You

usually thinks he is doing a good thing by making everybody behind him drive below the speed limit.

After a two-week visit in Germany in 2005, I came to the conclusion that the Germans have found at least one way to beat Mother Nature at the road rage game. The German Autobahn has a number of sections where there is no speed limit. This means that trucks and other slower vehicles drive in the outside lane at speeds of ninety to one hundred kilometers per hour, while cars drive in the center lane (if there is one) and/or inside lane at speeds exceeding two hundred kilometers per hour. When you experience traffic on the Autobahn, it isn't your own speed you notice. It is the fact that you are passing vehicles in the right lane at a speed difference of over one hundred kilometers per hour. On the Autobahn if someone in the inside lane attempted to match speeds with a truck in the outside lane they would be fatally rear-ended within minutes.

If Mother Nature has managed to find any "inside-laners" in Germany they didn't live long enough to create much road rage.

Back in the United States we have highway construction areas where the outside lane is closed, beginning one or two miles ahead. Now if everyone would obey the signs and begin merging into the center and inside lanes where indicated, traffic would continue to move near the posted speed limits (usually forty or fifty miles per hour). Three lanes would become two lanes long before reaching the point where the outside lane is actually closed, and everyone would be slightly inconvenienced with only a few minute's delay. But Mother Nature always seems to find a few folks who consider themselves so "special" that they don't have to merge like everyone else. Instead these folks race down the outside lane until forced to stop by the last row of orange safety cones. Then they force their way into the line of moving cars making everyone stop to avoid a collision.

The result is a traffic jam that typically extends for miles and moves at three or four miles per hour. Everyone except for those "special folks" has to wait for almost an hour to get through. Most of us N's can expect to experience more than a few "inside-laners" and at least one construction traffic jam during an average five hour trip.

Newton & Einstein, Stuff They Didn't Tell You

On one rare occasion a pickup truck driver and I managed to get the upper hand at one particular construction site in North Carolina. In an effort to prevent those "special folks" from using the outside lane to get ahead of the rest of us, this pickup truck edged partially into the outside lane while trying to keep his place in line. I could see what he was trying to do, so I edged even further over to the right behind him. Together we effectively blocked the outside lane. The car behind me noticed all this and was nice enough to hold our places in line. As a result, a number of "special folks" were trapped behind us. It wasn't long before the lines of cars began to move much faster because no one was cutting in further down where the orange cones were.

The mystery is that I've never again seen that technique used effectively.

N's need to be careful in their selection of clothing. Here is a partial list of clothing an N should avoid:
- Ski mask if you live in Miami,
- Steel toed shoes (airport metal detectors love these),
- T-shirts with slogans that encourage overthrow of the U. S. Government,
- Jackets that bulge like you might be carrying a weapon or worse,
- Sweatshirt with the logo for a U. S. Nuclear Weapons Laboratory if you are traveling in Iran or North Korea,
- Red baseball cap that says "Make America Great Again!" on it.

What are some other ways we can cope?

First, let Mother Nature have her fun and don't take her antics too seriously. Maintain a sense of humor. I know it's difficult, but remember Mother Nature won't do you any serious harm, unless you inflict it on yourself. One technique is to assume that whatever is happening is just an adventure in virtual reality. No matter the frustration, pretend the consequences aren't real, or at least not significant in the long term. Ask yourself, if this was a video game and you had nothing to lose would Mother Nature's little tricks really bother you that much?

Newton & Einstein, Stuff They Didn't Tell You

Another idea is to start your day with Plan B rather than Plan A. N's know that Plan A rarely works out, so why spend any serious time on it. Put all your effort into Plan B and start with that instead. If Mother Nature isn't paying close attention you may actually get away with something.

It's worth remembering that there's always a small chance she hasn't realized you are aware of her.

Yet another way of staying sane is by taking advantage of the fact that Mother Nature can get overextended. If you happen to catch her when she is stretched too thin, you can setup a friend who's also an N to take some of the heat off of you. Subtly arrange to place your friend in a situation you know Mother Nature can't resist, maybe one of those frustration in public "two-for-one" deals. You can judge how successful you've been by noticing how aggravated your friend becomes compared to your own circumstances. If it looks like he is worse off than you, then self-congratulations are in order.

Of course one sure way to maintain your sanity is to surround yourself with other N's who Mother Nature likes to abuse even more than you. But there are some problems with this approach.

The first problem is finding more than one or two people who fit this description. The second problem is convincing them to associate with you. And then there are the long-term effects of continued association with these people. You many find that you've simply traded frequent frustration and confusion for permanent depression.

Obviously this solution is not for everyone.

Extended warranties are a good idea for N's and a waste of money for Y's. Mother Nature has significant influence when it comes to things mechanical and electronic. That means N's should expect things to fail and should not expect that they will able to fix them. That's exactly why extended warranties were invented. It's like buying "insurance" in Blackjack when the Dealer shows an Ace (N's should always do that too). If you're an N it's worth paying a few extra

Newton & Einstein, Stuff They Didn't Tell You

dollars for the piece of mind that comes from knowing at least some of Mother Nature's pranks won't hit your wallet.

There will be days when you'll wonder if a miracle has occurred overnight and you've been transformed into a Y. Relish those days when they happen. Remember the old saying "Make hay while the sun shines". There will also be days when Mother Nature's pranks are particularly brutal. If she really gets to you, acknowledge her talent. Stop, give a respectful look toward the sky, and say "Good One!" Sometimes things will get better, sometimes they won't.

One thing that never works is begging for mercy. Mother Nature doesn't know about pity. She interprets begging as a clear sign of weakness, and just heaps more on.

I wanted this chapter to provide at least one tried and true coping method that absolutely works for everyone. Unfortunately none has been identified to date. This is probably due to three things:
- Most N's are justifiably reluctant to admit their plight to anyone but themselves, let alone admit they need help.
- There is a very large tolerance in society for those who live on the edge of insanity (i.e., only N's that suffer to the extreme, like Al Bundy, actually get noticed).
- To her credit, Mother Nature is extremely innovative and constantly finds previously unidentified ways to punish us N's.

It's sort of like trying to catch a terrorist who never follows a pattern. The clues are there but, just like the CIA and FBI, no one seems capable of connecting the dots ahead of time.

Actually, paranoia is considered "politically correct" these days, so who's going to care if one more person acts like some unseen force in the universe is screwing up their lives.

Newton & Einstein, Stuff They Didn't Tell You

Chapter Ten
Great Expectations (NOT)

Insanity: doing the same thing over and over again and expecting different results." - Albert Einstein

Most Type Y's lead a relatively routine, even dull, life compared to Type N's. If you are a Type Y:

- You buy something and it works the way it should right out of the package.
- Problems with your car are usually found at the garage during routine maintenance or an oil change.
- When the instructions say "Some assembly required", all the parts are actually included in the package.
- New software loads onto your PC and performs exactly as described in the owner's manual.
- If you ever do need to call the "Help Desk" for a computer problem, the first person you talk to knows how to fix it.
- The Federal Tax Code and Software License Agreements are straightforwardly written in plain English.

These and many other similar experiences lead a Y to expect good things. Y's learn to expect success and they typically get what they expect.

Type N's see the world differently. For them life is infinitely more varied and challenging.

For example:

Newton & Einstein, Stuff They Didn't Tell You

- Repairing a new purchase to make it work is par for the course.
- Cars, including rentals, break down on the highway (at night or on Sunday), not in the garage.
- "Some assembly required" means you have to fabricate one or two missing parts out of hair-pins, paperclips, wire coat hangers, etc. (That's why you keep that coffee can full of old nuts and bolts.)
- Loading new software requires multiple attempts, and involves conflicts with other software or your virus protection; deletes or replaces some of the drivers that came with your computer (and you don't have the original CD); and can't be uninstalled without leaving behind some "files that may be used by other applications", which you don't have the guts to delete.
- When you call the "Help Desk", the first, second and third (you never get the same person twice) "experts" enthusiastically describe corrective procedures that can't be performed or don't work, after you finally convince each of them that the problem you are having is actually possible.

These experiences persuade an N to expect difficulty, frustration, and sometimes failure. This becomes self-fulfilling; N's typically learn to expect what they get.

People in today's highly engineered world have learned to expect certain conventions (no, I'm not talking about the kind where you can get drunk on company time and charge it to your expense report).

Among these are:
- Water faucets that turn counterclockwise to open and clockwise to close.
- Light switches that are down for off and up for on.
- Automobile gearshifts where "Reverse" is to the left of "Park".
- Clothing that zips or buttons from the right for men and from the left for women.
- Doorknobs that turn clockwise to open, but deadbolt locks that turn clockwise to lock.
- Car doors that are hinged at the front, not at the rear,
- Automated Teller Machines (ATM) located on the driver's side of the car, not the passenger side.
- A sliver of lime when you order a Corona (imported beer).

Newton & Einstein, Stuff They Didn't Tell You

I attended meetings in several government buildings in the Washington, DC area where the faucets in the restroom actually turned clockwise to open and counterclockwise to close. I had great fun watching people (obviously N's all) coming out of the restroom with the front of their suits all wet. If you have ever installed a set of "three-way" light switches, you know it can get pretty confusing. Even if you install them correctly, it's still impossible to know whether up is on or up is off for any of the switches. Normally this isn't a problem, except when the light bulb burns out. You would like to know that the circuit is off before reaching into the fixture to replace the bulb.

Thanks to Mother Nature you need a voltmeter, and maybe an electrician to know for sure.

If you decide to give up your car with an automatic transmission in favor of a sporty two-seater with a six forward speed stick, you will soon discover that "Reverse" isn't to the left of "Park". In fact there is no "Park" at all. And "Reverse" is all the way past the six forward speeds to the far right. Y's seem to make the transition fairly quickly; N's seem to take a little longer, probably because they're worried that Mother Nature has some really sinister trick to play on them here. I actually have a men's jacket from Pebble Beach that buttons left over right but zips with the left hand. It confuses me every time I put it on. Some of the better hotels (the ones where N's usually stay) have deadbolts that turn counterclockwise to lock.

Several cars are made with doors that hinge at the rear. When I was about eight years old my parents owned a 1949 Plymouth with rear doors that hinged at the rear. Since there were no seatbelts in those days, I always sat in the back seat when we went anywhere. During one trip to see my aunt, my father turned to my mother sitting in the front passenger seat and asked if her door was ajar. I thought he was talking to me. I reached over and turned the door handle on the rear door. The next thing I remember was getting up off the dirt along side the road. The car was stopped about one hundred feet away and my parents were running back down the road to see if I was alive or dead. Doors that open into the airflow and yank you out onto the road are not a good idea for us N's.

Newton & Einstein, Stuff They Didn't Tell You

I know of an ATM machine in Maryland that is located on the passenger side. Maybe it was intended as a joke just for us N's. About one time out of three when I order a Corona at a restaurant I have to ask for the lime.

Whether you are an N or a Y, when you ask a question you expect to get a response that makes sense. Only a few years ago this was not very difficult. If you had a question about your telephone bill, utility bill, credit card statement, etc. you simply dialed the phone number on the statement. When someone answered the phone you asked your question, and kept asking questions until you got an answer(s) that was satisfactory. If that didn't work you could go to the telephone company office or the bank and ask your questions face to face.

No one realized what a privilege it was to talk to a live person, until suddenly they were all gone.

In the 21st Century if you have a question you MIGHT get to talk to a live person if you have the memory skills to navigate through a half-dozen or more multi-layered and interconnected voice-menus. Anyone who has ever tried this knows how easy it is to get "lost in the system". Instead of asking your question, you find yourself answering questions posed by a computer-voice with very limited vocabulary and no interest whatsoever in hearing what your problem might be.

If you persevere, you eventually get to the menu option that says "All our representatives are busy helping other customers. Your call is very important to us. Someone will be with you in a moment. This call may be recorded for quality assurance purposes." (That last statement is supposed to convince you that someone really cares). This is typically followed by music that repeats itself until only an exorcism can remove it from your head.

The brainwave activity of a person put in this situation rapidly drops to zero; i.e., the person is essentially brain dead. However as long as the battery on your phone doesn't also go dead, you have a fifty percent chance of talking to a live (in the broadest sense possible) person.

Newton & Einstein, Stuff They Didn't Tell You

You also have an equal chance that sometime during your wait that obnoxious music will suddenly be replaced by a dial tone. You know what that means. Yep, you get to start all over. And don't think that you can get around all this by going to the office and talking face to face. The telephone company stopped providing offices you can walk into many years ago. They have no intention of letting you interact with a live person face to face.

How does the experience of dealing with phone voice-menus differ for Type Y's and Type N's?

First of all, Y's simply don't have to call their phone company, utility company or credit card bank as often as N's. Mother Nature arranges for Y's to enjoy a much higher percentage of correct billing statements than N's. Second, if a Y does have to make such a call, their question is likely one that the computer-voice can readily answer. That's because Y's have questions that are predictable (like their lives) with answers that can be programmed into the computer-voice. A Type Y may only have to go two or three levels deep into the voice-menu to find the answer they are looking for.

Type N's on the other hand usually have questions that weren't predicted by whoever programmed the computer-voice. Thus, N's must talk to a live person if they have any hope of getting an answer that's useful. The "live persons" that work for these companies are aware that almost everyone that reaches them is an N.

Given this knowledge these "live persons" assume that:
- Any answer they give the caller will be received like a box of chocolates,
- Their answer doesn't have to be correct, because the caller won't be able to reach the same "live person" again to complain,
- They get paid the same whether they give out good answers or bad ones,
- Type N's don't expect to be successful anyway so what does it matter if their problem gets solved or not.

One thing you can definitely expect if you are an N is discrimination.

Newton & Einstein, Stuff They Didn't Tell You

No, it's not the kind of discrimination where you can sue your employer, or the government to get the money you need for early retirement. That's because it is impossible to prove in a court of law. Nevertheless, it is definitely observable if you are an N.

Some examples of people and institutions that discriminate against N's include:
- Schools and colleges (public and private)
- Automobile Dealers
- Financial Advisors
- Stock Brokers
- Tax Auditors
- Banks/Mortgage Lenders
- Interstate Highway Designers
- Grocery Sackers

You may have noticed in high school or college that N's were the last to finish those grueling multi-hour exams. It's not because they don't know the material, and it's not because they are slow. The reason N's are the last to finish is because they know that Mother Nature has mischievously embedded mistakes in their work and they need the extra time to find them. Based on the principle of Invisible Mistakes, their search is in vain but they try anyway. As my father used to say "Even a blind hog finds an acorn once in a while". Usually time runs out before they do in this case. Of course the teacher or professor who is scoring the exam will spot the invisible mistakes immediately.

And that is where the discrimination comes in.

Teachers learn to spot the N's in each class fairly quickly. It's the inverse of the "Halo Effect", reserved for the brightest Y's in the class who automatically get A's on all their exams because they have been labeled as "A Students". Conversely N's are branded as slow and prone to errors. Thus the teacher knows to give their exam papers extra scrutiny, otherwise known as "discrimination you can't prove".

Newton & Einstein, Stuff They Didn't Tell You

For similar reasons, automobile dealers usually give lower trade-in allowances to N's, financial advisors spend less time explaining why your portfolio isn't growing like the Dow Jones Average, Stock Brokers don't warn you about those "risky" stocks, Tax Auditors pour over your tax return for as many days as it takes until they find your mistake (it's got to be there somewhere), and Banks/Mortgage Lenders downgrade your credit report based on pure suspicion of financial incompetence, all because you are an N. Grocery sackers also put fewer items in each grocery bag if you are an N.

Fewer items per bag means more bags for you to struggle with.

Mother Nature obviously had a hand in developments designed to discriminate against specific groups:
- Commercial airline seats were designed to cause excruciating back and neck pain for people over six feet tall.
- Chinch bugs were created to frustrate those who like lawns of St. Augustine grass.
- Telemarketing was invented to frustrate people who have telephones.
- Chocolate was developed to frustrate people who are trying to lose weight.
- Ferrari's are built just to frustrate car enthusiasts who can't afford one.
- The Master's Golf Tournament is played every year just to frustrate all the golfers who live in the Augusta, Georgia area and, therefore, can't get tickets.
- Major League Baseball umpires live to frustrate Major League Baseball fans.
- Screaming two-year-olds exist just to aggravate everyone else in the restaurant.
- Supermodels and fashion magazines were created just to frustrate normal women everywhere.

Politics is more difficult than physics." - Albert Einstein

Newton & Einstein, Stuff They Didn't Tell You

Funding for government contracts is another example of expectations that can be deceiving, and in this case Mother Nature has some powerful allies inside the Capitol Beltway in Washington, DC. Those of us who have worked on government projects know that every year each contractor has to submit a Scope of Work (SOW), a Project Schedule and a Project Budget. These documents tell the government specifically what tasks can be performed (SOW) over what period of time (Schedule) and for how much of the taxpayer's money (Budget). In the real world there is a rigid relationship between these three documents.

For example:
- Less money means less work can be done on the same schedule, or
- Less money means the same amount of work can be done but it will take longer (i.e., schedule will stretch out), or
- Shorter schedule (less time) to accomplish the same work requires more money.

Here's where expectations become important.

In spite of the documents provided every year by their contractors, the government always expects to reduce the project funding (money to the contractor) and still get the same SOW (work) done in the same time (schedule). It does this by authorizing the documents provided by the contractor, and then a few weeks later taking away some of the money it promised to provide. In the commercial world this would be considered a breach of contract. In the government sector it's just considered being tough with the contractor.

In theory any project that survived a previous funding cut can always be cut again with no adverse consequences.

It's sort of like airlines that routinely overbook flights by ten percent or more. They know they don't have enough seats but when you show up and can't board the flight they simply apologize and promise not to do it again, year after year. Except there is a difference in government contracting. Less money means employees have to be "downsized" (we used to call it being laid off or fired). But

Newton & Einstein, Stuff They Didn't Tell You

government contractors aren't allowed to "downsize" unless the government approves. If it is an election year (and sometimes if it isn't) the government won't give its approval.

That's like telling the passengers who have tickets, but no seats, to ride on the wings.

All of this is right up Mother Nature's alley. She loves to find your breaking point. Over time this situation is analogous to trying to drive from Washington, D.C. to New York City once a year, but each year you're allowed less gasoline than the year before. The first few years you may be able to tune up the engine to get better gas mileage, or take less luggage to lighten the load. But eventually there is nothing more you can do. And the government doesn't believe you when you call to say you've run out of gas in New Jersey.

You won't find a Win-Win scenario for this situation in Chapter Eighteen. Our government believes they can force contractors to operate more efficiently by giving them less money year after year. Said another way "The flogging will continue until morale improves". Perhaps, like thermonuclear war, the only satisfactory solution is not to play the game. And that is why many companies refuse to bid on government contracts.

Anyway, I'm sure you're comforted by the knowledge that our nation's weapons grade nuclear materials are stored and protected by contractors operating under this kind of pressure.

Newton & Einstein, Stuff They Didn't Tell You

Chapter Eleven
Computing Your Odds

As far as the laws of mathematics refer to reality, they are not certain; and as far as they are certain, they do not refer to reality." - Albert Einstein

When you work with electronic stuff you have to consider the odds that it will do what you want. Mother Nature's favorite electronic device is unquestionably the personal computer. Ever since she, Steve Jobs and Bill Gates first conspired to control the world with these things, us N's have seen life get tougher and tougher.

Most of the civilized world has already been seduced by PC's in much the same way that Mickey Mouse was tempted to wear the Grand Wizard's hat in the Sorcerer's Apprentice. However, in this case Silicon Valley has no intention of coming to our rescue to prevent flooding the world.

The flooding is intentional and right on schedule.

At first we're all mesmerized by our PC's powers to make life easier. But gradually you find you are working for it, instead of having it do things for you (e.g., when your computer starts asking you to answer its questions instead of answering yours). Then it starts automatically updating its own software, accessing your bank account to pay your bills, selecting which online shopping sites you prefer, and downloading who knows what from the Internet while you're asleep.

Newton & Einstein, Stuff They Didn't Tell You

Suddenly, one morning you turn it on and discover things have gotten out of control.

It has learned so much about you that it's paying your bills before you wanted them paid. It's rearranged your schedule to be more efficient when you didn't ask it to. Some of your information has been archived (your computer decided you didn't need it anymore because you weren't accessing it often enough). Plus there are four new software programs running to give you instant weather forecasts, stock market figures, biographical sketches of singles in your area, and ten new songs you can download for free.

It's the information age and Mother Nature wants to be certain you can't get the information you're looking for without expending maximum effort to separate the wheat from the chaff. She also knows that if you're drinking from a fire hose you're bound to swallow something you didn't mean to once in while. Some Internet sites put "cookies" in your computer so their computer can find your computer again later while you're asleep. Some even include "spy ware" that can report back to them all sorts of information that you didn't want to share. When you download something visible to your PC you're usually getting lots of invisible stuff you don't want as well. Your personal computer now has the stuff you put on it plus lots more stuff that other people wanted to put on it too.

It's kind of like sharing your gym locker each day with an ever-growing number of strangers.

For the first time in history, people now have direct access to more information than anyone could possibly digest in one hundred lifetimes. The price of admission for most of us is anywhere from $600.00 to $2000.00 depending on whether you want to buy a portable (laptop) or desktop computer and how many bells and whistles you're willing to pay for. Recall that Mother Nature likes to separate N's from their money as often as possible. She and the computer manufacturers have recently found another subtle way to do that. It's called a "rebate". Since companies began offering rebates, the price you see at the store is not the price that rings up at the cash register. (Actually all the cash registers are

Newton & Einstein, Stuff They Didn't Tell You

now computers, too. Isn't it interesting that it takes a computer to sell you a computer?

Perhaps in the near future the human part of the sale won't be necessary. Computers will be able to buy their own computers without the middleman.)

For example, the average rebate on a laptop is about sixteen percent, $250.00 on a computer priced at $1500.00. When you pay for the computer, you pay sixteen percent more than the price marked on the showroom floor (e.g., $1750.00). Then you get home, fill out all the paperwork, attach the receipts, and mail it all off. In about eight weeks you get a check back for the extra $250.00 you paid at the store. In actuality, you have just given the computer manufacturer a $250.00 interest free loan for eight weeks.

Multiply your loan times two-thousand people a month and the computer manufacturer enjoys $1 million in continuous interest free capital. And it's all at your expense.

The operating software (e.g., Windows 10) and the applications software (e.g., Microsoft Office) for your PC must be updated every few years. Actually, the existing software runs just fine and does everything you need. Plus after about a year you've finally learned how to use it to do what you want. So why update it?

Here are the major reasons:
- Just like car designers, computer software designers would be out of work, if they couldn't periodically reshape things and put the "new" label on them.
- Hackers would run out of things to do if new vulnerabilities weren't introduced with each new software update (all the old vulnerabilities eventually get exploited and then patched, in that order).
- Computer hardware makers would be out of work without new software updates designed not to run on the hardware you have.
- Computer training personnel would lose their livelihood if the software features everyone has grown accustomed to weren't rearranged to confuse experienced users.

Newton & Einstein, Stuff They Didn't Tell You

- Like any life form, personal computers must continue to evolve and expand their influence across the planet. (I can't predict the year when the Internet will become self-aware, but when it does you can bet it will extract payback from all us carbon-based life forms.)

There are those who are sufficiently clairvoyant to see what's coming. They're called "computer experts". These people have already aligned themselves with the invading organism so as to become the "chosen ones" when computers take over the world. They speak an ancient language, and sometimes meet and converse in a secret place by the same name, called "DOS".

WARNING: anyone trying to go to "DOS" without knowing the magic words is doomed. Even escaping from the gates of "DOS" can be tricky for us mortals. The Gate Keeper for "DOS" is Mother Nature's first cousin.

In the early days of computers, Mother Nature discovered that software programs sometimes get into fights with one another, called "conflicts". Most modern software keeps these conflicts invisible to the user. That way we can't figure out who's fighting and just turn one of them off. In fact the only way we know when one of these conflicts occurs is that our PC freezes, i.e., stops doing anything visible. We can move the little pointer around, but clicking on stuff is a waste of time. If this happens you can hold down the "CTRL", "ALT", and "DELETE" keys all at the same time. Sometimes you will then get a message telling you that the program is not responding (no shit!).

Many times the only way out of this dilemma is to turn your computer off, losing whatever changes you've made since you last saved your work. (Taking away its supply of electrons will get a stalled computer's attention every time.) Then you restart the computer and pray that whatever happened before doesn't happen again.

Some software also likes to hog certain hardware and refuses to share. If you use a particular communications port on your PC to access the Internet you may be surprised one day with a message telling you that this port is in use, even though you're not using it. Mother Nature just played a little joke on you. Some software

Newton & Einstein, Stuff They Didn't Tell You

you loaded recently wants to hold on to your communications port continuously just in case it needs it sometime. You can turn that program off if you can find out which one it is. If you talk to a computer expert, he'll likely tell you to meet him in "DOS".

But you don't know the magic words.

In the old days (1990's) if you had a high-speed Internet connection you probably noticed that your "high-speed" (very slow by today's standards) modem would lose its mind periodically. After several episodes with your Internet Service Provider's help desk you eventually learned how to reset it without much difficulty. Mother Nature always preferred the slower dialup connections to the Internet; they were much more fun. Unlike the high-speed connection, the dialup connection sometimes "broke" without warning. And because it was much slower, downloading a Microsoft patch, a picture of Aunt Lucy, or other large file took a significant period of time. If you are an N you could count on your dialup connection "breaking" whenever you were downloading a large file. You could also count on the interruption coming with only twenty seconds left to complete a fifteen-minute download.

Remember Mother Nature loves repetition and the principle of Maximum Effort.

Mother Nature also had a hand in designing computer memory. For that reason, if you accidentally delete an important file, it's practically impossible to recover it (unless you happen to be one of those computer experts we talked about). But if that same file happens to be one you desperately wanted to erase forever from your computer, then the FBI, the CIA and several other Federal Agencies can recover it no matter how many times you erased it.

The term "user friendly" depends on the user, one more instance of discrimination against us N's. When the Apple Computer Macintosh model was introduced it allowed the user to interface graphically using a point and click approach. The revolutionary thing about these machines was that, for the first time, all the "computer program language" was hidden from the user.

Newton & Einstein, Stuff They Didn't Tell You

I recall hearing two comments about this machine:
- "The good thing about the Macintosh is that it does everything for you." – mostly from N's who were satisfied or intentionally ignorant of how the computer got things done.
- "The bad thing about the Macintosh is that it does everything for you!" – mostly from Y's who preferred to control how the computer got things done.

Of course when Microsoft introduced the Windows Operating System some time later the other half of the population was hooked. The invasion had begun. Clearly this was a red-letter day for Mother Nature.

Mother Nature used to really enjoy turning off the power when us N's were pressing hard to make the deadline for some important document. You could tell who the N's were when this happened. Heads would suddenly become visible above the cubicle walls like prairie dogs peeking out of their holes on a vast grassy field.

Whoever had lost the most data was the first to speak, as though the rest of us weren't in similar pain.

Then everyone went out and bought uninterruptible power supplies, also known as batteries. This spoiled Mother Nature's fun (temporarily) so she invented the "hard drive crash". This is where you turn your computer on and it stares back at you like a deer in the headlights. Your hard disk will not spin, which means you have no operating system, which means you're screwed if you haven't backed up your work on some memory device other than your computer.

N's learn (painfully) to backup their work about every twenty minutes to multiple memory devices. Y's never learn this valuable skill, but then they have no need for it so no harm done. Over the years, memory devices have become smaller and smaller while simultaneously expanding their memory capacity. This means that instead of misplacing a five inch floppy disk with a single forty page report stored on it, you can now lose a 128 gigabyte piece of plastic the size of your

Newton & Einstein, Stuff They Didn't Tell You

thumbnail that has several decades worth of reports, pictures, graphics, financial records, etc. Something that small can fall between the cushions of the sofa or into the toilet (they aren't waterproof) and it's gone forever.

Remember the law of Mischievous Attraction is stronger for things of higher value.

Then software designers began to conspire with Mother Nature to provide functionality you didn't want. For example, my money management software saw me enter a check that I wrote to a credit card bank. Immediately it started asking me questions (now who's working for who?):
- Account number, etc.?
- Name, address of financial institution?
- Current balance?
- Expected monthly payment (same or different amount each month?)?

All I wanted to do was enter a check I wrote. But the software wouldn't let me until I answered all of its questions first. Then next month when I wrote another check to the same bank my computer asked me if this was my regular payment or something different. Now I'm sitting here telling my computer to mind its own damn business.

Just let me enter the check, please!

Unless you happen to be the software designer who wrote the program, how your computer does what it does is invisible. That gives Mother Nature an infinite landscape to populate with stink bombs, bear traps, land mines and anything else unpleasant she can come up with. As an N you have a choice. You can avoid all of this by moving to a desert island, remaining isolated from the rest of the world (no more Facebook, Twitter, Whats App, etc.) and all its resources (Amazon, Google). Or you can recognize that no matter how Mother Nature stacks the odds against you your personal computer will occasionally do what you want it to, and when it does it's well worth the effort.

Newton & Einstein, Stuff They Didn't Tell You

The first decade of the 21st Century brought computer software and hardware changes that must have pleased Mother Nature immensely. Every new operating system upgrade produced by Microsoft introduced a greater number of failure modes and vulnerabilities to viruses, malware, etc. It wasn't long before you needed anti-virus software (at additional cost), which further slowed down whatever you wanted to do. As new PC system upgrades alternated between better, and then worse, than it's predecessor, frustrated users began to look for alternatives. Apple computers seemed to offer better and safer options. Whether Mother Nature had a hand in Microsoft's loss of market share is not clear, but the added complexity of all computer systems provided ever-increasing opportunities for her to make life more difficult for all us N's. To add insult to injury, PC owners had to pay for the Microsoft upgrades that made their computers less user friendly and run more slowly. At least you got a CD containing the software updates, so could reinstall as many times as needed. All that changed as personal computing moved into the second decade of the 21st Century.

Imagine how thrilled Mother Nature must have been as she watched computer hardware designers systematically eliminate hardware options that users had always relied on, in a quest to make PC's lighter and thinner. Sometime in 2008 it became obvious to us N's that the majority of problems with our computers could no longer be corrected by getting help from the "help desk" or "technical support representative". And then things started going wireless. But Mother Nature extracted a price for letting us get rid of those cables - a plethora of new ways your computer could suddenly find itself disconnected from the Internet. Computer software had also become so complex that no one, not even the programmers who wrote it, could make it work properly. Mother Nature must have been thrilled: an infinite number of failure modes with no solutions in many instances, other than to reload the software, or even buy a new computer. Time for Microsoft to take a new approach - issue future upgrades, wait for users to find the bugs, and then issue patches. Downloading patches became a monthly exercise if you owned a PC. Apple computer users had it a bit better. The upgrades were free and loading them was painless.

Newton & Einstein, Stuff They Didn't Tell You

In April 2010 Apple began selling a tablet (iPad), smaller than a laptop and without a keyboard or USB port. Others, including Microsoft, soon came out with their own tablets, but none have been as successful. Now we had laptop computers and tablets, as well as smart mobile phones (that came on the market back in 2007). Always thinking about backup plans, many of us N's decided we definitely needed to have all three, just in case Mother Nature should decide to make one of them fail to work properly just when we need it. Now that's three (or more) devices that need upgrading (updating) every few months.

Sometime in 2014 Mother Nature secretly alerted PC manufacturers to the idea that they could make laptop computers even thinner if they eliminated the CD drive, thereby making all our software CD's obsolete and usable. This also appealed to software designers, as an opportunity to sell their products to everyone all over again. Better still, they could make everyone download their software directly from something called "the cloud", adding another something they could sell - online storage for all our music, documents, etc. You could now update everything, including the operating system every few years, all wirelessly of course. Microsoft got the bright idea (from guess who?) that customers would rather 'lease' their "Office" software rather than actually buy it; something called "Office 365". Just like leasing a car, you could drive it but you didn't actually own it. And just like leasing a car, each time you got a new one all the controls had been moved around so that driving became a completely unfamiliar experience all over again. The learning curve for MS Office turned out to be about two years; guess how often a new version was issued? You guessed it!

N's soon discovered that having all their data conveniently backed up and stored on "the cloud" was great, until they lost their connection to the Internet. Mother Nature popped the champagne cork whenever that happened. Now she could put every single file you own out of reach for as long as she liked, just by killing your Internet connection in any number of enigmatic ways. She can even trick you into doing it to yourself, just by convincing you it's time to change your cloud ID or password. N's have discovered that the simple act of changing your cloud ID initiates a sadistic sequence of events so devastating that even the senior technical support representatives cannot tell you how to resolve it. They

Newton & Einstein, Stuff They Didn't Tell You

have all your files safely locked away from you, and they refuse to reveal the secret of how to get at them. Mother Nature must surely be having an orgasm every time that happens!

Newton & Einstein, Stuff They Didn't Tell You

Chapter Twelve
Games of Chance

Born losers; another way of describing Type N people!

By this time you have probably realized that Type N's have at least one thing going for them. They rarely become compulsive gamblers. That's because even the most compulsive personality has to win once in a while to stay hooked. And N's quickly learn from bitter experience that the term "born losers" was invented just for them.

The rare exception is where Mother Nature lets you win several times in a row just to enhance the frustration you feel when you lose it all back later. That's right – she sucker-punched you! Type N's don't become compulsive gamblers because they know the normal laws of chance don't apply when they're involved. Let's take poker for example.

I have from time to time participated in several types of poker, with my favorite being a game called "Texas Holdem". For those who've played poker, you know that you don't always need to get good cards. You can still win by simply betting as though you have a good hand (i.e., "bluffing"). A key element of this maneuver is that at least a few of the other players have to believe that you might actually have a good hand. Once everyone discovers (or already knows) you are an N, your ability to bluff becomes almost nonexistent. At that point in the evening the only way to win a hand is to actually have good cards.

This is where Mother Nature has her fun.

Newton & Einstein, Stuff They Didn't Tell You

Type N's who are brave enough (or dumb enough) to play poker discover a curious paradox. They excel at having the second best hand at the table. They often have good cards (by the normal laws of probability) and are therefore reluctant to discard one of these "good" hands without betting something. I recall being lucky enough to get "pocket aces" (best possible dealt hand) on three occasions at Texas Holdem one particular night. I lost to a Queen high spade flush, a Jack high straight, and three Kings (the third King was the last community card dealt – the "river card"). The most fun for a Y is to win over an equal hand held by an N based on a higher "kicker".

If I only had a penny for every time I've seen that.

To check out this problem of having second best hands, I decided to play against the casino poker game on my home computer. I didn't win a single time but I had the second best cards nine out of twenty hands. Twice I was dealt a pair (Kings and Jacks), but lost both times. That's conclusive evidence for me. Playing solitaire against your computer is no less frustrating than playing against a Y. And here's one more data point. I believe I currently hold the record for the most games of computer solitaire played in a row without a win, that being twenty-nine games on February 14, 1998.

Games of chance are one of Mother Nature's clever ways of rapidly separating N's from their money. Type N's play poker until they have exhausted the money they brought with them. Since this takes significantly less time than for the other players, they then get to watch for the rest of the evening and marvel at how different their "luck" is compared to the Y's. If the pain of watching gets too great they can simply go home early. This doesn't work of course if the game is at your house and you have to play the gracious host/hostess until you can get everyone to leave. If you are the host and your boss is playing, the evening can become more uncomfortable than a root canal without anesthetic.

A similar, but less costly, experience involves people who play Contract Bridge. Most suburban bridge clubs include players of varying skill levels. In fact some players consider bridge parties a social event and spend most of the evening

Newton & Einstein, Stuff They Didn't Tell You

talking about anything but bridge. In bridge it is difficult, if not impossible, to "bluff". You have to get good cards in order to play a contract, just as you must have possession of the football to score a touchdown. While you can also score points by defeating your opponent's contract, who wants to spend the entire evening just playing defense.

Type N bridge players usually don't get much practice at playing to win the contract. But when they do, like in poker, they discover another curious paradox. For N's, the opponent playing behind them (i.e., on their left) always has the higher cards (e.g., a King over your Queen, Jack over your ten, etc.). Trying to win a contract by finessing your opponent's higher card only works if you are a Y. Type N's know this and don't risk a finesse because they know it's not going to work. Type Y's have a distinct and observable advantage over N's at the bridge table for this reason, and because they usually get all the face cards.

But you can't comment about that fact at the table. The Y's just won't understand why you're whining.

Mother Nature likes some sporting events more than others. She also likes some teams more than others. This includes specific football teams, baseball teams, soccer teams, etc. If you aren't convinced just take notice of how many interceptions, fumbles and other mistakes occur during a high stakes football game. Usually these are not evenly split between the two teams. One team seems to get more than their share. That team will often get more than half the penalties as well. Sports commentators like to blame this on a lot of different factors. I suspect there's only one "factor" involved. And we know who she is.

Consider how rich you would be if you knew which side Mother Nature was cheering for on any particular afternoon. It's almost as good as having an advanced copy of next week's newspaper before the Stock Market closes. Sorry to say this isn't going to happen. But you can do something else that is almost as good. Gather up as many N's as you can find and get them to bet on the game. Then look to see which team the majority of them bet on. That's right; you go bet on the other team. Now you've got Mother Nature over a barrel. The only way

Newton & Einstein, Stuff They Didn't Tell You

your team can lose is if the team most of the N's bet on wins. Mother Nature is loath to let that happen, even if it means letting you win one.

Congratulations! You've just discovered one of the ways to beat Mother Nature at her own game. We'll talk more about that later in Chapter Twenty.

Never bet against Mother Nature one on one. She controls the odds. She'll beat you like a rented mule. Find games of chance that involve other people's money as well as your own. If you have to play, that's the way to do it. Remember; as long as all the N's in the world don't bet the same way, some of them have to win some of the time. It's the only chance you've got, so take it.

Of course there are some games well suited for N's. My favorite is chess. Chess is very deliberate game where random (or even non-random) chance has very little to do with the outcome. It involves analyzing a great many alternative moves, and requires innovation when your opponent does something really unexpected. This game is perfect for N's.

In fact most Y's don't have the patience or ability to constantly reanalyze their next several moves, which is a requirement for playing chess. Another game for N's is the oriental game of "Go". Go is a game of placing small stones (round playing pieces) on a board (grid) in such a way that you surround your opponent's stones to capture them. The rules for Go are incredibly simple but developing strategies that will win the game can be excruciatingly difficult, even for experienced players.

Some of us consider fishing to be a "game of chance". You make your wager (buy a boat, trailer and some fancy fishing gear) and cast the dice (or monofilament line in this case). If Mother Nature is mad at the fish that day, you may catch a few. Otherwise, it's a grand excuse to spend some quality time in the fresh air and enjoy the sound of water lapping against the side of the boat.

Some fishermen, in an obvious attempt to tilt the odds in their favor, have invested in Global Positioning Satellite (GPS) systems and electronic fish-finding equipment. Each boat looks like the bridge on a nuclear attack

Newton & Einstein, Stuff They Didn't Tell You

submarine. But Mother Nature loves electronic stuff. She'll have them fishing over the hospital waste disposal site in no time. Besides, she favors that ten year-old boy (especially if he is a Y) fishing with a bobber and a live minnow. If anyone's going to catch a fish it's going to be him.

I recall one summer day my oldest son (remember he's a Y) and I were fishing from a canoe in a cove. He was eight years old at the time. We had been fishing for about an hour when something hit his minnow and ran off fifty feet of line before he could tighten the drag. He wanted me to take the reel but I wouldn't touch it. It took him about twenty minutes to get that fish up to the boat. Out of the water came a bass weighing over six pounds. By the time we got it into the boat we were already surrounded by four $15,000.00 fishing boats all wanting to know what bait we were using. Nobody caught another fish in that cove the rest of the day.

If you really want to roll the dice against Mother Nature, go duck hunting. This is where adult human beings sit for hours in tiny little boats or huts over freezing water in February sometime before dawn. The object of the game is to wait for a flock of ducks to fly over so you can jump up and shoot them. The only problem is that when you finally see or hear the ducks, your body is frozen to the point that you can't stand up, much less shoot a gun. This is because Mother Nature likes ducks. You're just not going to shoot one without suffering numbing cold and excruciating pain for a minimum of two hours. I spent a lifetime waiting for ducks one cold February morning in east Texas.

I recall promising God that if he would deliver me alive from this cursed place I would never try to shoot a duck again. He did and I haven't.

Remember that Mother Nature loves and protects animals, especially when threatened by us humans. Hunting and fishing are real bargains for her. She can frustrate us at the same time she's protecting them. And she's given them the ability to recognize N's and Y's. If you are an N, just accept the fact that the twelve-point buck or ten-pound bass you want to hang over your mantle has the advantage of being able to spot you a mile away.

Newton & Einstein, Stuff They Didn't Tell You

It might make returning home empty handed a little less painful.

Newton & Einstein, Stuff They Didn't Tell You

Chapter Fourteen
Packaging your Frustration

Mother Nature gained control of the packaging industry nearly half a century ago. Ever since then products have been sealed in clear plastic shapes designed to frustrate the most determined consumer. Unfortunately, this particular malaise affects both Type Y and Type N people equally.

Packages that say "Press here to open" will open from almost any location except that one. It all started with those wax-pasteboard half-pint milk cartons in school lunchrooms. These things never opened on the side that said "Open". But they would open easily from the other side. I remember my Latin teacher in high school said, "What you teach your children your land becomes". She was right. We are a nation of people who know how to buy stuff but not how to get it out of the package when we get home.

Plastic packaging nowadays is tougher than Kevlar, especially on small high-value electronics. Even a sharp knife won't cut through some of this stuff. Manufacturers say these packages are designed to make it hard for shoplifters to open products in the store and take the contents unnoticed. OK, so if you plan to shoplift something, you'll need an acetylene torch, bolt cutters, and a diamond-bit saw.

Newton & Einstein, Stuff They Didn't Tell You

I have a portion of my shop dedicated to opening packages of electronic stuff I've bought. Sometimes it takes half an hour.

Then there are those things you buy in shrink-wrapped packages that tell you if you return them they must be in the "original packaging". Only problem is you can't get to them without destroying the "original packaging" in the process. And the message about having to return them in their "original packaging" is hidden inside the "original packaging".

Mother Nature can be pretty clever sometimes.

If you order something online it may be shipped to you in a box filled with Styrofoam peanuts. Somewhere in there is the thing you ordered. You just have to dig through all the mess to find it. Soon you have Styrofoam peanuts all over the floor and it becomes obvious that pouring part of the box into a plastic trash bag is the solution. But Mother Nature designed Styrofoam peanuts not to pour, especially not into a plastic trash bag that won't stay open. Now you have even more Styrofoam peanuts all over the floor, and you are no closer to finding whatever treasure is hidden in the box. In one final desperate move, you grab the box and dump what's left in it.

There, stuck to the bottom left corner is your prize. It isn't broken and it also isn't what you ordered!

Many brands of soft drinks come six to a package, held together with clear plastic webbing. Not only is this clear plastic webbing a danger to wildlife when it ends up in the landfill, it is also a source of frustration for us humans. If you take the plastic soft drink bottles out of the webbing you find they won't stand up on the refrigerator shelves without falling over. If you leave them "webbed" together so they will stand up, you have to take the entire six-pack out of the refrigerator every time you want to pull one bottle free of the others. And pulling one bottle free is no easy task. Once you do get it free be careful which direction you point it when you open it. If you use a knife to cut the bottles free from their webbing be careful to not puncture the bottle.

Newton & Einstein, Stuff They Didn't Tell You

I've reached the point where I will only buy soft drinks that don't come in this type of insane package.

Clothing can be equally challenging.

Why do the makers of dress shirts feel compelled to fold them up and stick pins in them? You don't have to buy other shirts that way. And every dress shirt maker has to hide a different number of pins in different places. That's so you can't be sure if you've gotten all of them out. You'll find the one(s) you missed when you put the shirt on for the first time. Then there are all these little pieces of plastic and cardboard around the collar. You could run a bulldozer over the shirt collar and not mash it flat with all that stuff in there. And let's not forget the paper that gives the package that crinkly sound when you pick it up in the store. Are they afraid we won't buy their shirt if it doesn't make that crinkly sound?

Sock makers put that crinkly paper in their socks for the same reason, I suppose. But why put it in only one sock? Why not both of them? One sock has to make noise, but the other one doesn't?

So now your new shirt is free of pins, plastic, cardboard, crinkly paper, etc. Because of the way it was packaged you also have to wash it and iron it before you can wear it. (I tried ironing a new dress shirt without washing it first – the ultimate exercise in futility!). Finally, two hours later you have a new shirt you can actually wear.

Wouldn't it have been much easier and cheaper (for them and you) if they had just sold the shirt on a hanger?

Mother Nature also invented childproof caps for bottles of medicine, mouthwash, etc. She did a really good job of marketing these things, too. Most of this stuff tastes so bad, no child would dream of eating or drinking it. Actually childproof caps are a mean trick played specifically on old people: excuse me "senior citizens". If you want hard proof, hand any one of these containers to a

Newton & Einstein, Stuff They Didn't Tell You

four-year old and then to someone over the age of sixty. The four-year old gets it open in five seconds but it takes the senior citizen almost a full minute.

Or how about these little cups of chocolate pudding with the aluminum foil lids that peel off? Aren't the lids supposed to peel off in one piece? They always tear down the middle when I try it. Try getting the remaining piece of aluminum foil off without getting chocolate pudding all over you.

Mother Nature also designed toilet paper rolls so that the leading edge is well camouflaged and glued down. Why is this necessary?

Toilet paper rolls are packaged in a paper or plastic wrapper to keep them from unrolling until you need them. Why, then, must the leading edge be glued down? And why are the "sheets" of toilet paper only about four inches long between perforations. Is anyone really going to use only one four-inch sheet? What's the harm in leaving a loose leading edge so we don't have to waste the first ten sheets trying to get the roll started? And why is this all designed to happen under circumstances where you are not likely to ask for help.

Two-inch wide transparent plastic packing tape is one of Mother Nature's award winners. Sooner or later you will lose control of the leading edge. When you do it immediately reattaches itself to the roll becoming absolutely invisible (Malicious Attraction). The only way to find the edge again is to carefully run your thumbnail around and around the roll until you feel a little bump. Now that you've found the edge, getting it started again is another challenge. This tape is designed to be very strong when wrapped around a package but very weak along its width. It's designed that way so that when your thumbnail finally lifts a small part of the edge of the tape and begins to pull it away from the roll you can only get a small sliver of tape to unroll. In fact you can get almost an infinite number of slivers, but never the complete edge you wanted. Now you have a roll of tape with many little starts and slivers, all of which are just as invisible as the original edge you started with.

Practically new rolls of this kind of tape end up in the garbage because there is no way to find a complete leading edge once it has been lost.

Newton & Einstein, Stuff They Didn't Tell You

Music CD's and movie DVD's are also packaged to be "consumer hostile" (that's the opposite of user friendly).

First you get the clear plastic wrapper off. It looks like the case should open, right? Wrong. Next you need to carefully peel off the little white bar code strips down each side. They look like they should come off in one piece but instead it's like peeling an orange. Finally you have your CD or DVD in one hand and little tiny pieces of sticky white plastic all over your other hand. Be careful not to get any of those little tiny pieces of sticky white plastic on your CD or you may ruin it and maybe your CD player as well.

What fun!

Over the past few decades Mother Nature has been secretly replacing prices (that you could read) with bar codes (that only a computer can read).

Try it. Walk into a store and pick up an item. There's the bar code but you won't find a price anywhere. That's because manufacturers have decided (with a little nudge from Mother Nature) that only their computers need to know the price. You're just the poor guy who's paying for it. Why should you need to know how much it costs? Let's take this a little further. Will automobile dealerships simply display a bar code on each new car, instead of the window sticker that lists the options and the actual price? How about houses? Will the real estate catalogs show pictures of houses with bar codes instead of the prices, street addresses, etc.? What if the price gets reduced? Will there be a bar code with a line through it, followed by another bar code that represents the lower price?

I keep meaning to buy stock in companies that sell portable bar code readers. Very soon everyone will need one to carry around shopping. Or maybe cell phones and tablets with come bar code readers built into them. Wait, they already have, almost. There's something called a 'QR code', and there are apps for your phone or tablet that will read them. Unfortunately the QR code doesn't tell you the price of the product. It only takes you to the website that selling it. But perhaps in the future you will be able to take a picture of each car you look

Newton & Einstein, Stuff They Didn't Tell You

at, record the bar code (revealing price, options and dealer's invoice, etc.), and transmit all of this to your best friend (via Facebook, Twitter, etc.) using a single device.

All the commercials on TV will be converting to bar codes as well. But you won't need your bar code reader for that. The human eye should be able to memorize the bar code for $19.95 in only a week or two.

Of course future generations eventually won't need bar code readers.

When I was in school we learned the native language (English) and one "foreign language", usually Spanish, French or German. I suppose my great grandchildren will be taught "Bar Code" as a "foreign language" regardless of what country they are born in. If (when) computers take over the world, computerized school teachers can then teach "Bar Code" as the native language. Humans will only need English, Spanish, French or German if they want to talk to each other.

Several decades ago I recall attending a seminar that predicted major shifts in how manufactured goods would soon be marketed. As a consumer I began to wonder how these marketing shifts could affect the survival of certain companies. About half way through the seminar the speaker made some rather extreme (at least to me) statements. He said, "Car manufacturers and car repair shops are necessary, but new car showrooms are not. Books are necessary, but book stores are not. Clothing makers are necessary, but clothing stores are not." He was referring to the notion (now being realized) that these and many other products can be purchased over the Internet without having to leave your living room.

This was not good news for the sales personnel at Macy's, Sears or Barnes & Noble. The guys that staff the Cadillac, Mercedes and BMW showrooms weren't too happy about it either.

It was good news for companies like Federal Express, United Parcel Service, DHL, and even the postal service, because it meant more and more stuff would have to be packaged and delivered to your door. New companies, such as

Newton & Einstein, Stuff They Didn't Tell You

Amazon, have sprung up with no physical storefronts on Main Street, just enormous warehouses outside the city. In recent years Internet purchases have risen to the level that the Christmas sales data our government and the news media use to judge the health of our economy has to be "adjusted to account for online shoppers" who elect not to battle the traffic Friday after Thanksgiving. In fact the Christmas shopping data isn't complete until online sales on "Cyber Monday" have been factored in. Of course Mother Nature loves online sales because there are so many more ways things can go wrong for you online, compared to simply walking into a store, paying for your new shirt, and arriving back home with it, all in the space of half an hour.

Mother Nature has such clever ways of making life more complicated just when we thought it was going to get simpler.

When UPS delivers your order it's now up to you to open the package. Just like Indiana Jones, you may need some knowledge of ancient hieroglyphics to get your treasure out of the box unharmed. And if it isn't what you ordered or doesn't fit, it's up to you to repackage it and ship it back to the online store you ordered it from. The online store may require you to talk to a sales representative (who has a few questions) to get a "return authorization number and label" to place on the package you want to return. They can also tack on additional handling charges and even a restocking fee for your returned item. Since they already have your credit card information, they can add whatever charges they deem appropriate without your consent. Even if the packaging didn't frustrate you, it's a guarantee that the return process will.

Here are few more packages that Mother Nature can arrange for you:
- Free all expenses paid vacation for two in sunny Florida or the Bahamas (you spend the entire three days watching real estate videos).
- Free vinyl siding for your house if you can convince five of your neighbors to buy it for theirs.
- A $39.00 per year warranty contract (i.e., $195.00 paid up front) that covers your computer for the next five years, which is two years beyond when it becomes junk.

Newton & Einstein, Stuff They Didn't Tell You

- Buying insurance at the Blackjack table when the dealer shows an Ace (always a sucker bet).
- Free installation of a natural gas line to your residence, if you agree to purchase a new gas furnace from the local gas company.
- Two of almost anything advertised on TV for the original price of one, but only if you call within the next sixty seconds.
- "A $160.00 value for the incredibly low price of just $19.95".
- Credit cards that advertise only five percent interest for the first six months, then charge you twenty-one percent for the rest of eternity.
- Corporate mergers where the acquiring company agrees not to lay off the current staff, then cuts their salaries in half only twenty-four hours after the merger documents are signed.
- Retirement packages that go into default five years after you take them, because the company used its retirement fund to hide revenue losses from the stockholders.

One last point. The banana comes in a great package, durable, tamper proof, and yet easy to open. Why can't the packaging industry learn from the banana?

Newton & Einstein, Stuff They Didn't Tell You

Chapter Fifteen
Timing is Everything

Mother Nature isn't always able to make the wrong things happen. Sometimes she has to settle for just making things happen at the wrong time.

Have you ever noticed that the telephone rings just when you are at a critical point in some task that can't be stopped. Again, let's use cooking as an example.

Let's say you are preparing hollandaise sauce and you are right at the point where you have to keep stirring the mixture to keep the emulsion from separating. Mother Nature arranges for a friend who hasn't spoken to you for three months to call at precisely that moment. Of course, the friend has some complex problem that only you can help her with, and she has to resolve it right now. So you sacrifice the hollandaise sauce and spend the next two hours on the phone helping your friend solve her problem. If this happens only once a year, you are probably a Type Y person.

If, however, your second and third attempts to make hollandaise sauce are similarly interrupted, either you have too many needy friends or you are a Type N, or perhaps both.

If you are an N, you've become accustomed to getting interrupted at the worst possible times, and usually for reasons that turn out to be trivial. Mother Nature

Newton & Einstein, Stuff They Didn't Tell You

also arranges for the phone to ring or a knock at the door when you are in the bathroom, especially if you are expecting an important phone call, or a package from UPS or FedEx that you have to sign for. (Most deliverymen quietly park just around the corner on your street and wait for you to leave the house or go to the toilet.) Mother Nature knows the importance of timing, and somehow manages to distract you just when your son hits that home run, or catches a touchdown pass.

If you are an N, you have to be very selective about when you try to get things done.

For instance, years of experience has taught us N's that trying to drive a golf ball straight and long off the tee has the following odds:
- 20% that you will hook the ball
- 20% that you will slice the ball
- 10% that you will top the ball and watch it go bouncing along the ground off the tee
- 5% that you will ground the club-head before making contact with the ball
- 1% that you will miss the ball entirely.

That leaves a forty-four percent chance of hitting the ball in the direction you want it to go.

However, driving the ball straight and long while your boss, family member or anyone else you want to impress is watching is much more difficult. That's because Mother Nature has the opportunity to get "two for one", i.e., she can frustrate and embarrass you both at the same time.

The approximate odds then become:
- 33% that you will hook the ball
- 33% that you will slice the ball
- 20% that you will top the ball
- 9% that you will ground the club-head
- 4% that you will miss the ball entirely.

Newton & Einstein, Stuff They Didn't Tell You

If you do the math you can see that the odds of hitting the ball straight and long in this situation are only slightly better than zero. That's because even Mother Nature isn't perfect. She always has to leave you some chance, small as it may be, to make that one good shot every time you play. If she didn't, you wouldn't keep coming back to chase that little white ball every week and golf courses would go out of business.

Just remember that timing is everything. If you want to play well don't try to do it when someone whose opinion matters is watching. And don't expect to have a witness when you hit that hole in one either.

Mother Nature likes to intervene in your life when she catches you working against the clock. It's 11:00 PM on Christmas Eve, the ten-year-old is in bed, and now you have a new bicycle to put together. You only have until 6:00 AM. Under normal circumstances this job couldn't possibly take more than two hours tops.

Here's where Mother Nature helps you out.

First, you discover that all the nuts and bolts are metric, while all your box-head and socket wrenches are English. That's because Mother Nature arranged for your bicycle to come from France. You'll have to use those old adjustable wrenches so it will just take a little longer. Then you notice that the instruction booklet is missing pages 9 and 10, so you'll have to guess what to do with those parts not shown in the diagram on page 8 that are already installed on page 11. To make things more interesting there are two different size connectors both labeled as "Part 37B", and there is no "Part 37A".

Being an engineer, you are still confident that the ten-year-old will have a shiny new bicycle to ride long before 6:00 AM.

Next, you open one of the plastic bags of small parts and watch helplessly as two of the parts bounce across the floor and down the heating vent nearest you. One hour later you come up from under the house after disassembling and

Newton & Einstein, Stuff They Didn't Tell You

reassembling a significant part of your heating system to retrieve the missing parts. Then you notice that footnote on the parts list stating that the manufacturer has provided extras for these parts in case some get lost. I could go on, but I think you get the picture. The bicycle is finished just in time for the ten-year-old to come down the stairs and find it on Christmas morning.

And your mother-in-law makes a sarcastic comment at dinner when you fall asleep while carving the Christmas ham.

Timing can be important in sports. Have you noticed that a football team that could only complete eight out of twenty-three passes in the first fifty-eight minutes of the game can miraculously pull off nine sideline passes during the final two minutes? Why couldn't they do that earlier? They would probably be winning instead of losing. Mother Nature loves six runs scored in the ninth inning of the World Series baseball game, three "Hail Mary" passes in the last twenty seconds of the Superbowl, and birdies on the last three holes at the Augusta National on Sunday afternoon. It's her way of punishing the spectators who went home early.

Timing can also be an important discriminator in non-sporting events. The right thing done at the wrong time can be just as bad as the wrong thing done at the right time, or anytime for that matter.

Confused? If you send a box of candy to someone you love it's very important to know when to send it. If she's looking good in that new bikini, that box of candy will score points for your relationship. If she's thinking it's about time she lost a few pounds, that box of candy is not going to be welcome, and sometimes neither are you. So to make it up to her you invite her and another couple to go out dancing. Halfway through the evening she announces she's going to the restroom, and the other girl leaves to go with her. Why do women go the restroom in pairs or threesomes?

Suppose a guy announced he was going to the restroom and the other guy suddenly said, "I believe I'll go with you". Not the same thing at all, right? Timing is everything!

Newton & Einstein, Stuff They Didn't Tell You

Surprise is a great military tactic that was actually invented by Mother Nature. All ambushes work better if you don't see them coming.

Let's take an ordinary conversation. You and your spouse (or significant other) are talking about a friend who came over for dinner two nights ago. His name is Frank. You mention that Frank likes his new car, and she comments that she would have picked a different color. Then you say he wanted a minivan. It's perfect for taking the kids to school. Then she says that taking the kids to school wouldn't be an issue if he hadn't divorced his first wife.

Suddenly you're confused. Frank has never been divorced. Then she says it's all his fault. You're thinking what is his fault? And then it dawns on you. She is no longer talking about Frank. She's talking about someone else. So you go along with the conversation, hoping for some clue that will identify the "he" she is talking about.

Finally you have to ask the question, "Who are you talking about, dear?" To which she replies, "Haven't you been listening to me at all?"

The point of this little story is that women (and especially Mother Nature) like to change the subject unexpectedly, and with no warning. The fact that "he" is now someone entirely different from the "he" in the previous sentence is obvious (to them). There's no cue card that pops up saying "**SUBJECT CHANGE**". It just happens. You just weren't keeping up, right? Mother Nature likes to do the same thing, that is, change the source of your misery with no warning just to keep you off balance.

Let's consider the following example.

It's a sunny spring afternoon, a perfect opportunity to deposit that $450.00 insurance check in the bank. You just need to find your sunglasses. Fortunately you know right where you left them. Twenty minutes later you still haven't found them. Then you realize you don't know where you put the insurance check, either. **SUBJECT CHANGE** - forget the sunglasses, where in the hell did I put

Newton & Einstein, Stuff They Didn't Tell You

that check? A minute later the doorbell rings. It's the neighbor's kids. "Do you know your car has a tire that's almost flat?" they ask. **SUBJECT CHANGE** - now you've got to find out why your tire is going flat. That trip to the bank will have to wait.

Five minutes later the phone rings.

It's your son in Miami. He just got tickets for the AFC Playoff Game, but you'll have to leave in the next twenty minutes to make it in time for the kickoff. **SUBJECT CHANGE** - the flat tire will have to wait. You jump in your wife's car and head for Miami. And while your son is watching the big game, you are sitting next to him wondering where your sunglasses are, where you put that check, why did that tire go flat, and when is the wife going to go out and notice that you left her with no transportation?

One thing both Y's and N's look forward to is retirement. But here again timing is everything.

If you take your company's "early retirement package", perhaps at age fifty-eight, you may find that you don't have sufficient savings and investments to support yourself another twenty-five or thirty years until your death. On the other hand, if you work until age seventy you may have enough saved for a comfortable retirement but have too many health problems to enjoy it. Rest assured Mother Nature has the answer. She and hundreds of investment firms have designed lots of TV commercials to put your mind at ease.

If you just let one of these investment firms have all your money, they promise you will spend your "golden years" in paradise, just like that tropical Island shown on TV. That is of course unless the stock market doesn't perform up to their expectations, or your portfolio manager makes some bad decisions before he's fired, or the CEO of the company is caught in an insider trading scandal, or the company is bought by some bigger company who believes in a higher risk, shorter term investment strategy, etc., etc.

Newton & Einstein, Stuff They Didn't Tell You

For the same reasons that Y's seem to do better in the stock market and at the poker table, they also seem able to step right in to successful retirement. Y's get the "Golden Parachute", while N's usually get the parachute that fails to open.

Put another way, Y's get the gold mine; N's just get the shaft.

So when should an N contemplate retirement? You know Mother Nature isn't going to stop beating you up just because you've retired from your day job. And you know that most of the good part-time consulting jobs will be going to the retired Y's, who just want to replace their twenty-eight foot yacht with a thirty-six footer.

So how can you know what to do? The answer is simple. Work until you can't stand it anymore. Since you are an N, chances are this time is going to arrive before you are financially ready for retirement anyway.

Think about it. Which would you rather have – your sanity and not quite enough money, or enough money but nowhere in your padded cell to spend it?

Newton & Einstein, Stuff They Didn't Tell You

Chapter Sixteen
So What is Time?

People like us, who believe in physics, know that the distinction between past, present, and future is only a stubbornly persistent illusion." - Albert Einstein

What determines if a person is a Type Y or a Type N? Actually, it may have a lot to do with this thing we call "time." So what is time?

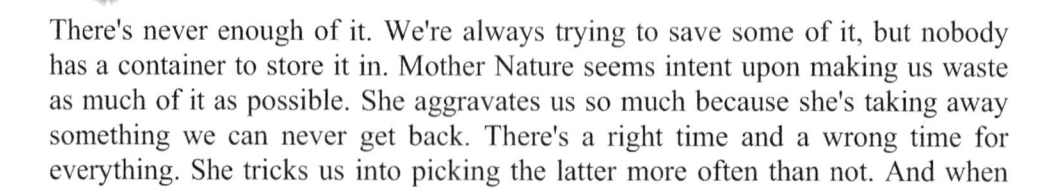

There's never enough of it. We're always trying to save some of it, but nobody has a container to store it in. Mother Nature seems intent upon making us waste as much of it as possible. She aggravates us so much because she's taking away something we can never get back. There's a right time and a wrong time for everything. She tricks us into picking the latter more often than not. And when

Newton & Einstein, Stuff They Didn't Tell You

the right time does come we aren't ready. Why does it take a long time to go someplace and a much shorter time to get back home (see Chapter 17)?

Time speeds up as you get older, making Christmas seem like yesterday instead of a year ago. Einstein insisted that time is relative. One of his famous quotes is: "Put your hand on a hot stove for a minute and it seems like an hour. Sit with a pretty girl for an hour, and it seems like a minute." Each of us judges the passage of time by how much we remember. As we get older we remember less and less; and so it seems to us as if time is speeding up (see Chapter Nineteen).

We use time to measure everything that happens; yet we can only observe it for one fleeting moment, which we call "now". We can sense time's passage, yet we can't see, hear, touch, taste or smell it. (Actually we loose all sense of it if we're sitting in front of a computer writing a book!)

If you have thirty minutes to eat lunch and I have thirty minutes to eat lunch, together we should have an hour to eat lunch, right? If I'm your teacher or your boss, I can give you more time (say, another twenty-four hours) to get that project completed or report written. Did someone else just loose twenty-four hours to make up for my bosses generousity? If I'm a Judge, I can give you more time in prison. If I'm your spouse and we've just had an argument, I can give us both more time to think about what we said to each other. If your fiancée needs time alone to think things over, you can give it to her. Time is like love; you can give away as much of it as you want without losing any yourself. But sometimes when you're out of time (or love), there is just nothing anyone can do to help.

If you think about it, you will realize that time only makes sense for "intelligent beings", i.e., living organisms that have memories. Rocks can't remember where they were five minutes ago or five centuries ago. Planets and stars exist from moment to moment but have no way to recall where they've been or how they formed. Only when we observe the motion of rocks, planets, stars and everything else around us can the passage of time be recognized. And actually the only way we recognize motion is by remembering that the rock was in a different location a few seconds ago from where we observe it now. We "sense" the passage of

Newton & Einstein, Stuff They Didn't Tell You

time by remembering that one event took place before or after another event (change and causality).

The only reason for time is so that everything doesn't happen at once." - Albert Einstein

Actually, maybe it does.

Maybe time doesn't really exist, but is only an illusion created just to make the life experience interesting for us "intelligent beings". In fact, what we observe as a dynamic universe with objects moving in all directions may be static, never changing. How is this possible? How could we "feel" the passage of time if nothing is actually changing?

Suppose the only thing that really exists is "now". And suppose each "now moment" is its own world, which includes a consistent past (memory) of what came before that "now moment" and a future that stems from that "now moment".

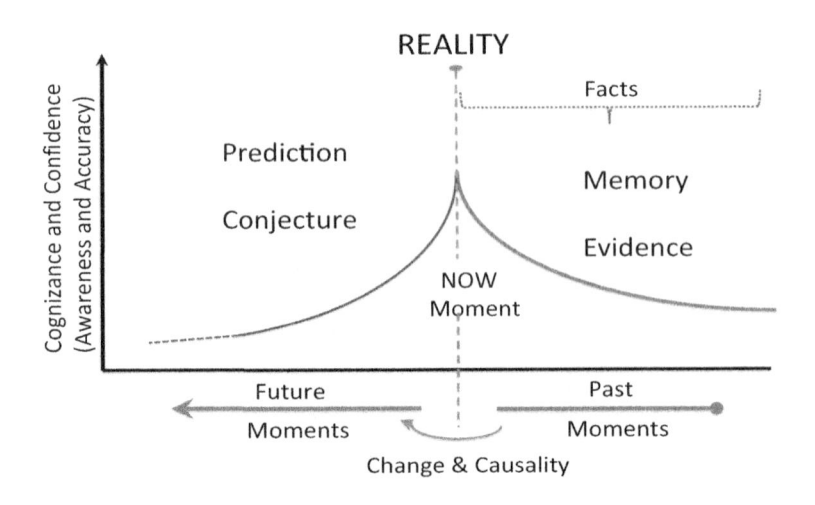

Newton & Einstein, Stuff They Didn't Tell You

According to the Heisenberg Uncertainty Principle, there cannot be just one "now". [Physicists like to talk about the Heisenberg Uncertainty Principle, which states that it is impossible to measure both the location and momentum (velocity) of subatomic particles at the same instant. Thus, there is always a probability of something happening, but never a certainty.] Instead of just one "now", there has to be a very large number of "nows", each one defining a complete past, present and future.

Actually there have to be enough "nows" to represent all your possible pasts and futures.

Of course we know from the laws of physics that some of these "nows" must be more likely (probable) than others. A "now" in which you fell off a third story balcony at age nine, then recovered to earn $10 million a year as a professional football player is not very likely. A "now" in which you played football in high school, attended college on a football scholarship, and then became a real estate agent is more likely. So who or what selects the "now" you experience, and how is that selection made? It may be a simple matter of probability. You have a better chance of ending up with a "now" in which you are a real estate agent than a "now" in which you throw the touchdown pass that wins the Superbowl.

"Nows" in which you are a famous rock star, U.S. Senator, or founder of a multibillion dollar computer software monopoly are pretty rare.

Here at last we may have a clue as to how some of us are Y's and others are doomed to be N's.

Y's may be the ones who happen to experience "nows" that are very probable (i.e., contain a larger proportion of expected and desirable outcomes). This leaves us N's with the "nows" that are less probable (i.e., contain a larger proportion of unexpected and undesirable outcomes). It may be that we are all initially subject to an unbiased roll of the dice in which Mother Nature has no say.

Newton & Einstein, Stuff They Didn't Tell You

But once the die is cast, Mother Nature immediately knows who she can go after.

At first it may sound as though once your "now" is selected then your past and future are predestined. However, this is prevented by the Heisenberg Uncertainty Principle, which guarantees each of us free choice (see Chapter Twenty-One). That means you switch from one "now" to a different (but similar) "now" each time you make a choice that results in only one of several possible outcomes (i.e., possible futures). And since each "now" comes complete with a past and future, each choice you make alters your past as well your future.

We are all used to the idea that our decisions can change our future, but the notion that a new decision can alter your past is a bit disconcerting. But if the past and the future are all embodied in a single "now", it's not so hard to grasp. The important thing to remember is that you are not aware that your past has changed, so all is still right with the world.

To you it seems like the same past you had all along.

If reality consists of jumping from one "now" to the next based on the choices we make, then perhaps it is those choices that define our identity. Suppose every choice you make is recorded somehow. By every choice I mean everything you chose to say and everything you chose not to say, everything you chose to do or chose not to do, every selfish decision, every sacrifice to benefit others, etc. Then the complete record of all those choices, large or small – easy or difficult, would become a unique statement that defines who you are.

The nice thing about this definition of who you are is that all the following things become irrelevant:
- Color of your skin, hair, eyes, etc.
- Gender or sexual orientation.
- Race or country of birth.
- Religious beliefs.
- University you graduated from.
- Personal financial success or failure.

Newton & Einstein, Stuff They Didn't Tell You

- Position on your company's Organization Chart.
- Language(s) you speak.
- Country, state, city or subdivision you live in.
- Every event in your life over which you had no control.

You can stop worrying about these things (especially the last one). A complete record of all your choices uniquely and unambiguously defines exactly who you are without mentioning any of them. In the end only your choices really matter.

Suppose your "now" is simply a set of memory data that is fed into your consciousness, with each specific memory carefully sequence-labeled as happening after some other event(s). A lifetime of memories could all be loaded at the same instant, but you would perceive every event as occurring in a sequence as they were labeled. In other words you would perceive that a period of time had passed.

Our actual observations only exist as a collection of 'Now' moments. The vast majority of what we are conscious of is made up almost entirely of short and long term memories of those observations.

For example, when you listen to music you are only hearing one or a few notes at any instant. Your consciousness remembers other notes in a particular sequence (as they were labeled) and interprets the result as a lovely melody lasting three minutes. But maybe all the notes (carefully sequenced-labeled) entered your consciousness together.

As it turns out, the memory data fed into our consciousness doesn't have to be particularly accurate. We all have experienced occasions where we remember something witnessed by other people as well. When we find others who can recall the sequence of events exactly as we do, then we are convinced it really happened. Watching a video recording of the events is even more convincing.

On the other hand, if everyone else recalls the event differently, we conclude that our memory might be incorrect. We often adjust that memory to agree with what

Newton & Einstein, Stuff They Didn't Tell You

the other people recall. People are convicted of crimes by a jury of their peers and spend years in prison based on this process.

In fact the past becomes what we remember, and what we remember becomes what we can get agreement on. For different groups of people the past is often converted by collective agreement to something other than what really happened. Sometimes these different groups spend a hundred or even a thousand years trying to annihilate each other as a result.

We often make reference to "an organization's past" or "their history". But if you think about it there can only be "your past". Let's see why.

What you "know" consists of events or conditions you have seen (heard, smelled, tasted, touched) yourself plus those events or conditions that others have told you about, either personally or in books, classrooms, TV broadcasts, photographs, movies, etc. You are most confident about the events and conditions you witnessed yourself along with others who agreed with your observations. You are less confident about events or conditions you witnessed if there were no other observers to agree or disagree. You are least confident about events and conditions you didn't observe at all, but someone else told you about them.

Was someone always with you to observe every single event and condition that you observed since you were born? Was this person also with you every time someone told you about other events and conditions you didn't personally witness? If not, then your "past" is unique to you. No one else has a past just like yours. You can tell other people about it but they can't share your actual memories.

Reality is merely an illusion, albeit a very persistent one." - Albert Einstein

Your past will always represent a reality that is unique to you.

Since your past is unique to you, Mother Nature might be able to change it anytime she felt like it and you wouldn't have any way to know the difference.

Newton & Einstein, Stuff They Didn't Tell You

She could change you from a rather common looking blond male to a stunningly attractive brunette female. If Mother Nature switched your "now" how would you know? Since your past is unique, no one else's past would be affected so they wouldn't know the difference either.

I used to have one of those "living aquarium" screen savers on my computer. You've probably seen them. The fish swim across the screen in such an incredibly lifelike manner that they actually seem to be living creatures. No matter how long you watch, their patterns of movement appear totally random. Their tails, fins, eyes, and mouths all move like living fish. They seem three-dimensional as they turn to swim in the opposite direction. They hesitate and change paths to avoid colliding with other fish, rocks or coral in the aquarium. They disappear behind rocks and coral or off the right or left side of the screen only to reappear exactly when and where they should. Except for the fact that they exist only in two dimensions, these fish behave exactly as though they are alive in a real water-filled aquarium. The software programming required to make these fish seem so lifelike is impressive.

If humans can write software that perfectly simulates the lives of two-dimensional fish, why couldn't a much more intelligent being create software that perfectly simulates (at least to us) the lives of three-dimensional creatures like ourselves. Such software would have to deal with three dimensions instead of only two, making it much more complex. This software would allow us to move at random (like the fish), avoid collisions with each other or solid objects (like the fish), and be limited to what we can observe of our environment (like the right and left sides of the screen saver aquarium).

But unlike the screen saver aquarium, software for three dimensions would have to provide us with much more complex interactions with objects (e.g., cars, computers, etc.), with our environment (larger than an aquarium), and most importantly with other humans. This would be very complex software, containing everything necessary to process our sequence-labeled memory data in a way that we perceive as normal consciousness?

Newton & Einstein, Stuff They Didn't Tell You

Have you ever considered the possibility that for each of us the universe may only exist as far as we can observe it at any moment? For the fish in the screen saver aquarium nothing exists outside the right and left sides of your computer screen. Those spaces are meaningless for them, just as any added dimensions beyond the three that we experience would be meaningless to us.

If our reality consists only of unique sequence-labeled memory data why bother with creating extraneous data to represent things that are outside our range of observation? If you happen to be looking up at the stars one night the universe would consist of your immediate surroundings on Earth, the person standing next to you, and as many stars as you could see with the naked eye. If you had a telescope more stars would need to exist in the area of the sky where the telescope was focused. But only the surface of the earth beneath your feet would need to exist, not the dirt and rock below, because you can't observe it.

If you are sitting in a restaurant looking out the window and across the street, for you the universe at that moment need only consist of the interior of the restaurant and the people in it, plus whatever is visible out the window. That means the young blond woman with the great looking legs walking down the sidewalk will instantly evaporate as soon as she rounds the corner and goes out of your line of sight and beyond your range of hearing. So will the cars passing by and birds flying overhead.

In fact nothing outside your range of observation (sight, hearing, smell, touch, and taste) needs to exist at all. The only way for that attractive blond to exist again is for you to leave the restaurant and chase after her. As soon as you turn the corner, she and everything else in your line of vision will instantly exist once more. But since you can't see the restaurant any longer, now it will vanish.

That could be bad if you left your fiancée sitting there drinking coffee.

For another example, consider the highway intersection that everyone complains about just south of your subdivision. Clearly a traffic light is needed there instead of just stop signs on the north and southbound lanes. As you sit at this

Newton & Einstein, Stuff They Didn't Tell You

intersection in the southbound lane waiting for a break in the east-west traffic you notice (if you are an N) something curious. The vehicles coming from the east are spaced just far apart that you never get a clear chance to cross. And then just as the eastbound traffic clears for a few minutes, the westbound traffic suddenly arrives to fill in the gap. It's as though someone is deliberately "orchestrating" all the east and west bound traffic so you can never get across.

Now such precise orchestration can't be easy (even for Mother Nature) since all of these vehicles started out from different locations, took different routes, traveled at different speeds before arriving at the intersection, etc. But consider how much easier Mother Nature's task becomes if you assume that each of the westbound vehicles is being created just out of sight over the hill to the east, and all of the eastbound vehicles are also being created just out of sight around the bend in the road to the west. Frustrating you to the edge of insanity turns out to be only a matter of creating a few hundred vehicles at just the right moments.

In fact some of them can be recycled and pass in front of you more than once if you're not paying close attention.

And here's one final example to consider.

Does everything cease to exist when you fall asleep, only to be recreated (in so far as you can sense) when you wake up? Haven't you noticed that some people seem to wake up in a different world (i.e., a different "now") every day? If reality is just a set of memory data then why keep generating that data when you are asleep? We all know that even the best computers have to shutdown for routine maintenance every so often. Maybe falling asleep is necessary to allow errors in your memory data to be corrected offline.

Doctors have found that a person's mental performance deteriorates when they are deprived of sleep for long periods. Maybe it's just that their memory data is overdue for offline maintenance. How about people who suffer from amnesia or blackouts? Did their memory data, or at least part of it, get permanently damaged or misplaced?

Newton & Einstein, Stuff They Didn't Tell You

Memory data should come with a "no questions asked" warranty. These people should get a refund.

There's one more interesting thing about how we perceive time. The memory data processed by our consciousness is always labeled as occurring before the present instant. This makes time appear to move in only one direction (i.e., the 'arrow of time'). But what if a memory gets mislabeled? If a memory is labeled out of proper sequence it can be very confusing (these are known as premonitions). On rare occasions a memory can get duplicated and a new sequence-label attached to the duplicate (this is known as deja vu).

And if someone (guess who) fiddles with one of your memories then that jeweler's screwdriver you saw in the kitchen drawer yesterday won't be there when you go to get it this morning (see Chapter Six). Even problems like the one experienced by Bill Murray's character in the movie "Ground Hog Day" may be possible.

Quality problems with memory data seem to be more prevalent for certain individuals (i.e., N's). Maybe Mother Nature is just a hacker on the grandest data network of all.

Indeed, the only evidence of time and space (i.e., reality) is that we remember things. Other people substantiate the vast majority of our memories to a very high degree of consistency, which convinces us that our memories really happened. But then if these other people are also part of the memory data fed into our consciousness, what else could you expect? Perhaps everything we see, smell, taste, touch and hear is only sequence-labeled memory data designed specifically for each of us, downloaded to our consciousness, and then erased.

Matter and energy, in fact the universe itself, may not exist at all (that would explain a lot!). Perhaps what each of us perceives as a lifetime is actually only an instant of data loading, processing and then erasure.

Newton & Einstein, Stuff They Didn't Tell You

That would mean you weren't really late to your niece's wedding, you only remember it that way.

One final comment on the nature of a software driven reality. As everyone knows, all software contains bugs. Perhaps concepts like "Dark Energy" and "Dark Matter", and our inability to reconcile Quantum Mechanics with Gravity all stem from errors in the software that makes each of us experience reality. In that event, physicists may never find the answers they seek.

For more information about this subject, read:

- Barbour, Julian, The End of Time – The Next Revolution in Physics, New York: Oxford University Press, 1999]

- Hawking, Stephen, Black Holes and Baby Universes and other Essays, New York, Bantam Books, 1993

- Hawking, Stephen, A Brief History of Time – Tenth Anniversary Edition, New York, Bantam Books, 1998

Newton & Einstein, Stuff They Didn't Tell You

Chapter Seventeen
Getting From A to B

Type Y people love to travel. That's because they (and their luggage) have a better than average chance of getting where they want to go. They even seem to arrive on schedule more often than not. [By now you must have realized that Y's have a better than average chance of succeeding at anything because Type N people pull the average down.]

Type Y's have one more reason to enjoy traveling. They never get lost. They always know where they are, even if they can't figure out where everyone else is. In their view, it's up to us to find them.

You've probably guessed that many N's would rather not travel if they can avoid it. Why? Because the travel experience gives Mother Nature an extraordinary number of opportunities to entertain herself, and always at our expense.

If you travel by car you should have a better chance of getting where you're going on time since you are the driver. You can take rest stops when and where you want, select the route you are most familiar with, and even change your itinerary at a moment's notice. Also, most drivers consider the risk of an accident to be lower because they are

Newton & Einstein, Stuff They Didn't Tell You

in control (i.e., driving), even though the accident risk of highway travel is actually one of the highest.

Nevertheless, many N's prefer to drive themselves rather than experience the joys of commercial air travel if their destination is within six highway hours, or maybe even eight. Here's why. You allow one hour for the drive to the airport, arrive a mandatory two hours before flight departure, spend two hours actually in the air, forty-five minutes to deplane and collect your luggage, then another forty-five minutes riding the bus to the rental car lot and signing up for your rental car. Now you've spent six and one-half hours if everything goes perfectly, which it almost never does because hundreds of people are involved and at least a few of them are guaranteed to screw up.

Driving yourself means that if there's a screw up, it's usually going to be your fault. And you deal with that every day.

For N's the problem with driving yourself is that now you are responsible for not getting lost. Like certain Interstate exits and Internet Websites, some roads shown on the map are like prehistoric tar pits. Y's seem to intuitively know not to go there, but Mother Nature sees to it that N's get to experience every one. These are the two-lane "shortcuts" that seem to get narrower and receive less maintenance the further you go, until you end up in a place that looks like a scene from the movie "Deliverance."

No one there can tell you how to get back to the "main highway." In fact no one there has ever seen the "main highway", or a dentist.

Y's consistently pass up the opportunity to discover the fact that "rural America" speaks a language that sounds only remotely like English.

One of the greatest inventions in modern times has to be the Global Positioning System (GPS).

Mother Nature must have been distracted by some other big government project (like the Star Wars anti-missile defense system) while the guys in the back room

Newton & Einstein, Stuff They Didn't Tell You

were quietly coming up with this GPS thing. Instead of trying to understand those maps created by Y's, now we N's can just tell the GPS unit in our car where we want to go and it will guide us there. They actually talk to you (in a sexy female voice), giving you step-by-step instructions on where to turn.

The beauty of the GPS is that it always (well, almost always) knows where you are. Then it tells you how to move from there to the next place you want to be.

There should be a similar device that gives step-by-step instructions for relationships, particularly ones where one party is an N and the other is a Y. A frequent problem for the N in these situations is not knowing where they are. And if you don't know where you are, it's hard to know in which direction to move next. Is she seriously interested in me? Was sending a dozen roses premature? Is three dates in two weeks overdoing it? Am I more than just "fun to be with?" What is she telling her girlfriends about me? Should I invite her to Jamaica for the weekend? One hotel room or two? The relationship GPS could tell you when to call her, where to take her for dinner, what to say, and what to wear, when it's time to introduce her to your parents, etc. It might even tell you if this is the girl you want spend your life with, or the one that just wants to spend your money.

Why couldn't those government guys with all those tax dollars come up with that kind of GPS?

Of course, if you have to travel long distances in a short time you have no choice but to fly. Commercial airlines are adopting new rules every day about the size of "carry-ons" and what you can't have in them. That means you have to let the airlines handle your luggage more often. And your checked luggage has to be unlocked so it can be inspected by total strangers. This is like inviting some guys off the street to come into your house while you're not home and look through your closet, underwear drawer, and bathroom cabinet to see if they can find anything they like. If something is missing when you get your luggage back, the airline can't tell you who might have taken it. If something has been added (like illegal drugs, etc.), the airline can't give you or the police any idea who put it there.

Newton & Einstein, Stuff They Didn't Tell You

What the airline can do is send you a letter three weeks after you get back home to let you know that they found a book of matches in your suitcase. The letter goes on to warn that if you let this happen again, they might refuse to let you travel with them in the future.

Commercial airlines are under a great deal of pressure to sell every seat on every flight. To do that, they have to overbook some flights, hoping that some of the ticketed passengers won't show up. Here's one way the airlines discriminate between Y's and N's. If you are a Y and your seat has been double booked, the airline upgrades you to Business Class or First Class at no charge. If you are an N and your seat has been double booked, the airline apologizes and attempts to find you a seat on a later flight. In fact that is probably how that lady ended up in your seat for the flight you were originally on.

The moral of the story: Y's get rewarded when the airlines screw up while N's get "inconvenienced."

Then there are those pesky weather delays. Mother Nature can control the weather where large populations are impacted. Some airports are notorious. Mother Nature's favorite airport is Atlanta Hartsfield-Jackson. From late March until early November, afternoon thunderstorms are a guaranteed daily occurrence. Travelers who live in South Carolina, Georgia, Alabama and Tennessee have a saying: "Try to die early in the morning, because whether you go to heaven or hell you will have to go through the Atlanta Airport to get there."

Mother Nature has some new opportunities if you happen to be traveling to another country. She works closely with the folks who screen your passport upon arrival. Let's take a British citizen who has just departed a ten-hour flight to the United States for example.

The conversation goes something like this:

Newton & Einstein, Stuff They Didn't Tell You

Agent - "I notice you applied for a Visa and were turned down."

Traveler – "Yes, the people at the American Embassy in London said I didn't need a Visa. I could stay in the United States for up to ninety days under the Visa Waiver Program. Therefore my request was denied."

Agent – "But we can't let you enter the United States under the Visa Waiver Program if you have ever been denied a Visa by the American Embassy."

Traveler – "So how was I supposed to know that BEFORE I requested a Visa?"

Agent – "That's not my problem. Please sit in this room for the next four hours while we decide whether to put you back on a plane to England. No, you are not allowed to contact the people who came to the airport to meet you. They will just have to wonder what happened to you. No, you can't have your luggage, which by now has been taken to some obscure location in the airport. England is one of our closest allies, isn't it? Welcome to America, and please stay awake for more questioning."

Not all destinations we seek can be found on a map.

Type N people can become Pulitzer Prize winning authors, Olympic Gold Medalists, movie stars, CEO's of major corporations, or even win a Nobel Prize in nuclear physics just as certainly as Y's. The difference is that N's have to work a lot harder to get there. And what's really wrong with that? My grandfather used to say "The harder the climb, the more impressive the view from the summit." For N's life is much more about the journey and much less about the destination.

Consider this example.

One couple (both N's) buys a new house. The first three years they work and save until they can buy a solid cherry dining room table with eight Queen Anne chairs, a matching buffet and china cabinet. A year later they can fill that china cabinet with eight place settings of fine porcelain from London. The next four years they save enough to purchase a black walnut canopy bed, matching chest

Newton & Einstein, Stuff They Didn't Tell You

of drawers and armoire. Five years later they convert the downstairs basement into a family room with a pool table at one end and widescreen TV with surround sound at the other end.

By the time their son is college age they are ready to convert his bedroom into a guest room or home office. Of course they could have done all of this much sooner if Mother Nature hadn't played a few pranks on them, like inviting the termites in for lunch one summer, the pine tree limb that put an eight inch hole in the kitchen roof during breakfast a year later, the fire that burned down the garage while they were visiting Aunt Sophie in Houston, and the City Council's three-year rezoning attempt that almost put a K-Mart next door.

A second couple about the same age (both Y's) also bought a new house. The wife's father helped out by providing a twenty-five percent down payment on the house as a wedding gift. One month after moving in, the husband's mother, not to be outdone, took the couple to Ethan Allen just to "look" at furniture. Six hours and $46,000.00 later "Mom" had purchased every piece of furniture the couple 'needed' to be happy in their new house. Four days later all the furniture was delivered and placed.

All the couple had left to do was walk around the house admiring all that life had bestowed on them.

So who had the richer experience? The N's worked hard and enjoyed years of planning and waiting as they saw their dreams gradually come true. Every item in their house is complete with memories of anticipation and sacrifice to share with close friends and relatives over the Christmas turkey.

The Y's got everything they wanted overnight. "Mom and Dad" made sure they had instant happiness.

It's always difficult to appreciate the destination when you didn't have to make the journey. Some Y's never find satisfaction in reaching their destinations because the journey was too easy or they skipped it altogether. That's why they obsessively search for new ones. In that sense Mother Nature does us N's a

Newton & Einstein, Stuff They Didn't Tell You

favor. She gives us those unbelievable experiences we can later tell our grandchildren about. She makes our journeys memorable (sometimes nightmarish) rather than just the shortest path to our destinations. Her persistent and infuriating interference in our lives can become in later years the stuff of family legend.

It's up to us to make it so.

None of us are born with the expectation of becoming a Pulitzer Prize winning author or Olympic Gold Medalist.

Our parents may have high hopes for us, but to accurately predict at birth who will be President of the United States or CEO of General Motors someday is virtually impossible. Yet no one ever achieved any of these positions without believing very strongly that it would happen. Somewhere between birth and adolescence most of us come to believe in a unique destiny. That belief stems from our experiences growing up, what our parents and friends tell us, what we see on TV and in the newspapers, and how we think our talents match up with our own needs and the needs of the society.

If your father, your grandfather and your great grandfather were all Marines, you may believe it is your destiny to join the U. S. Marine Corps. If your older brothers are all doctors, you may believe it is your destiny to become a brain surgeon. If you grow up in poverty and your older sister becomes a shoplifter and a drug dealer, you may believe it is your destiny to be a criminal. Being a Y or an N can affect how strongly you believe in your own destiny. Y's are more willing to go all-out in pursuit of their destiny because more of their childhood experiences have been favorable. N's are less willing to make such an all-out commitment because more of their childhood experiences have been unfavorable. It may be that many Y's achieve more success than N's simply because their belief in their own destiny is stronger.

In a very competitive world that strength of commitment may be all the edge they need.

Newton & Einstein, Stuff They Didn't Tell You

Chapter Eighteen
Paths You Did Not Choose

Isaac Newton's position, as Lucasian Professor of Mathematics at Cambridge University, is now held by Doctor Stephen Hawking. Doctor Hawking has written several books explaining the latest theories about the "Big Bang", how the universe was formed and how it behaves. It is a fact that none of these books mention the profound influence of Mother Nature. However, I refuse to allow that oversight to dissuade me, so let's push on.

One popular cosmological theory is that the Big Bang created not only the universe we observe but, in fact, an infinite number of universes. Some of these universes expanded so slowly that gravity stopped the expansion and they collapsed back into themselves before stars had time to form. Other universes expanded so rapidly that all the matter dissipated before it had time to coalesce into stars.

A portion of the remaining universes expanded at the right velocity to form stars but the stars all formed at the same time, burned out too quickly, and the heavier elements (e.g., carbon, oxygen, etc.) necessary for planets and life were never

Newton & Einstein, Stuff They Didn't Tell You

created. Some number of universes did manage to create stars that formed, exploded (supernova) and reformed to produce and distribute heavier elements across the cosmos, but conditions necessary for development of intelligent life just never happened.

Those universes may exist, but there is definitely no one there to observe them.

That leaves some fraction of those original universes (a fraction of an infinite number is still an infinite number) containing folks like you and me who get up every morning, get dressed and do whatever it is we do.

To be fair, in about half of those other universes all us Type N people could be Type Y people. And as a Y in another universe, when you flip a coin and call "heads" the coin should land "heads." That makes up for your experience as an N in this universe when you call "heads" and get "tails." Given an infinite number of parallel universes, every time you (as an N in this universe) flip a coin and don't get what you called, there must be another "you" (as a Y in another universe) who does get what he calls.

Stated more generally, all possible outcomes of every event must occur somewhere (even if there's no one there to observe them).

If an event produces one outcome in one universe, all other possible outcomes must simultaneously occur in other universes. That could mean that when Mother Nature seems to be making your life miserable in this universe, maybe she's really just making some Y happy in another. [Although an infinite number of parallel universes may exist as modern cosmology predicts, I'm not buying the argument that Mother Nature is fair minded. I still think she is a bitch at heart.]

One more point is worth making here. If the number of parallel universes is infinite, then indeed "you" must be living as a Y and as an N in equal numbers of universes.

The agony comes from knowing you can't voluntarily switch places (unless maybe you think you can survive the trip through a "Black Hole").

Newton & Einstein, Stuff They Didn't Tell You

If you were living as a Y in a parallel universe how would your life be different? Well, for one thing you would make different choices. That's because choices are based on perception of risk. And Y's perceive risk very differently from N's. Perception of risk is based on your own experiences plus what other people tell you. If you've ridden around in a car for the past sixty years and never been hurt, you probably perceive riding in a car as an acceptable risk. If someone you trust told you that a particular car was falling apart and the wheels might come off at any moment, you would probably perceive riding in that car as an unacceptable risk. Y's are more willing to take risks because their experiences have been good ones. Failures have been few and far between.

N's are less willing to take risks because many of their experiences have not been good. Fear of failure is real and ever present.

So what paths do the Y's choose? Y's choose paths that are adventuresome, often exhilarating. They buy stocks that promise a higher rate of return, unconcerned about losing all their money. They pursue careers where pressures are high but rewards are great. Y's are extremely competitive because they know they have the edge.

N's choose paths that are more conservative and safe. They put their money in bonds, and mutual funds, preferring high security over high return. N's pursue careers where perseverance and careful analysis are valued over quick judgment, and where a single mistake will not crush them.

Most N's know they don't have the edge and make life's decisions accordingly.

Now consider the possibility that, just like there may be an infinite number of universes, so there may be an infinite number of paths for each of us. And every decision we have made has selected one path among many from that moment forward. The Y that is you in another universe would be an entirely different person. Because, as a Y, they made different decisions, which lead them down different paths, which compounded like interest in a savings account.

Newton & Einstein, Stuff They Didn't Tell You

What about all the un-chosen paths, the ones we didn't take (at least in this universe)? Do they fan out from moments past like heat lightning in a summer night sky?

Did our alter egos actually take each of these alternative paths in other parallel universes? If we only live in this universe, do we care? If I hadn't gone back home for my briefcase one morning, all my remaining paths might have evaporated in one instant years ago. How would that have changed the lives of people I've known since that moment? Should I let those thoughts change the paths I choose from this moment on? If I had full knowledge of how each of my decisions will affect every aspect of the cosmos, would I decide differently?

Fortunately none of us can comprehend the totality of impacts from every decision we make. If we could we would be too overwhelmed and frightened to decide anything.

But each us is aware of some of the impacts each of our decisions will have in the future and has had in the past. Let's consider how we are able to make decisions at all. Each time we are faced with a decision we must consider both the past and the future. What we do in the next instant depends on what we remember (past) and what we want to happen next (future). We use our memories of past decisions and their outcomes to find a close match (if there is one) to the decision we are now facing. What did we decide then and was the outcome favorable? We use our knowledge of probability and sense of prediction to anticipate the outcome of that same decision in the future. Will the outcome be favorable under future circumstances that may be different from the past?

At the moment of choice we weigh all the "data" from the past plus our predictions of the future and decide.

Each of us believes that the past we remember actually happened, and that the future we predict will actually happen (for us). We don't sense that all possible pasts actually happened and that all possible futures will actually happen. But

Newton & Einstein, Stuff They Didn't Tell You

suppose (as suggested in Chapter Sixteen) the past and the future are just sequence-labeled "data" fed into our consciousness in a single instant, which we sense as "now." And we are switching from one data set to another every time we make a decision. All that is required for us to experience a consistent reality is that the past data and future data remain consistent at any moment.

As long as we don't see ourselves as a six-foot tall male with blond hair one instant ago and expect to be a five foot seven inch tall female brunette an instant from now, we're fine.

Contrary to what was suggested earlier, maybe you (as an N in this universe) can (and do) switch places with your alter egos living in parallel universes. Perhaps what modern cosmologists perceive as an infinite number of parallel universes is simply an infinite number of sequence-labeled data sets ("nows"), which encompass all possible outcomes of all possible events (past, present and future). You may not have to survive the trip through a Black Hole after all. But then, wouldn't it be great if you could shop around to pick just those sets of sequence-labeled data (i.e., "nows") that would make your life most enjoyable?

Actually, Mother Nature may be doing that for you. Only she isn't picking the "nows" you would pick. Considering the fun she is having, you have to ask yourself why would she ever hand you the remote control?

But let's get back to Doctor Hawking's universe (if it's really there) and what we can observe about it.

Not too many years ago another noted scientist, Doctor Edwin Hubble, characterized the universe as expanding in all directions at ever increasing speed. He came to that conclusion based on the fact that light coming from distant stars is Doppler shifted toward the red end of the visible light spectrum. And the more distant the stars, the greater the Doppler shift. In other words everything in the universe is accelerating away from a single point, which Doctor Hawking and others refer to as the singularity. All matter, energy and time itself are thought to have been created from the singularity at the instant of the Big Bang some 13.8 billion years ago.

Newton & Einstein, Stuff They Didn't Tell You

But several questions remain to be answered. How can anything expand forever? Why doesn't the force of gravity act to slow the expansion of all matter in the universe? Although it may still be expanding, the rate of expansion should be decreasing rather than increasing. Everything should be slowing down because of gravity. No one has yet observed direct evidence of a force strong enough to overcome gravity and make the universe expand at an accelerated rate forever. That hasn't stopped physicists, however, from inventing something called "Dark Energy" as a fanciful fudge factor to explain the unexplainable.

Suppose Edwin Hubble was wrong and all matter in the universe is not accelerating away from itself? Suppose it only appears to be accelerating because of the way we are forced to measure such motion from planet Earth 13.8 billion years after the Big Bang?

Suppose only a few of you really care whether the universe is really expanding exponentially or just faking us out? For those who can't sleep some nights and want to dive headfirst into the possibility that the theory of Dark Energy is quite definitely wrong, please see the essays at the end of this book.

In fact, only one thing can actually move at the speed of light and that is light itself. It follows that photons of light have no dimensions, but infinite inertial mass. No amount of additional energy can increase their velocity. And photons of light do not age, because at the speed of light time does not progress. Each photon of light actually spends zero time (from its point of view) in our three-dimensional universe. And if you could ride with that photon of light, you would discover that an almost infinite number of events in the universe all do indeed happen at once!

When we look through a telescope at a distant star, the photons of light striking our eyes have not aged even one second since they left the star millions or perhaps billions of our years ago. In a single instant these photons of light lose a billion years of immortality to become a tiny impulse registered by our retina and conveyed to our brain as an image of celestial majesty. What separates

Newton & Einstein, Stuff They Didn't Tell You

personal astronomy from all other scientific endeavors is the possibility that those photons were created for just that purpose.

To truly appreciate the cosmos, we must constantly remind ourselves of what they are looking at and how it is that we can observe it at all.

How does Mother Nature figure into the greater plan for the universe? It's my opinion that she is responsible for the scale of things. Without her influence, we might only have things as small as atoms and as large as our own Milky Way Galaxy.

Certainly that was sufficient to satisfy everyone up until a hundred years ago.

We now believe that there are subatomic particles too small to measure even with light of the shortest wavelengths. These are things small enough to follow the Heisenberg Uncertainty Principle, which you may recall is what gives us all free choice. And the cosmos apparently stretches for billions of light years in all directions and contains billions of galaxies like our own; so many that we can never look at them all.

Why create things too small to ever observe and too far away to ever explore?

Mother Nature's job is to surprise us when she can, frustrate us when it suits her, and most of all to keep us in awe of the life experience. You may not like Mother Nature's influence but you have to admit one thing. Mother Nature is never boring!

For more information about this subject, read:

Einstein, Albert, Relativity – The Special and the General Theory, New York: Barnes & Noble Books, (1920) Republished 2004.

Newton & Einstein, Stuff They Didn't Tell You

Filkin, David, Stephen Hawking's Universe – The Cosmos Explained, New York: Basic Books, 1997.

Rees, Martin, Just Six Numbers – The Deep Forces that Shape the Universe, New York: Basic Books, Perseus Books Group, 2000.

Wolf, Fred Alan, Parallel Universes – The Search for Other Worlds, New York: Simon & Schuster, 1990.

Newton & Einstein, Stuff They Didn't Tell You

Chapter Nineteen
Age Matters

The most aggravating thing about the younger generation is that I no longer belong to it." - Albert Einstein

A̲ge affects how matter behaves. I'm talking about YOUR age here, not the age of the object or device you're trying to work with. It could be a simple device like a zipper on your favorite jacket, or a complicated device like a digital camera. All matter in the universe knows how old you are and acts

Newton & Einstein, Stuff They Didn't Tell You

accordingly. This effect is hardly noticeable up until age fifty. But trust me when I say it becomes exponentially more obvious each year beyond sixty.

Here are just a few obvious examples:
- Button holes and eyes on needles become smaller
- Things fall on the floor more often (due in part to "gravity waves") and end up further away when you reach to pick them up
- Any task that used to require 4 or 5 attempts to achieve success now requires 6 at age sixty, 7 at age seventy, etc.
- Mechanisms stick more often (door handles, cabinet drawers, etc.)
- Online accounts stop accepting valid passwords, and procedures for resetting passwords become more complicated
- Gravity increases at unexpected moments (i.e., when you're getting up from the chair/sofa)
- Shoelaces and toenails become unreachable
- Invisibility, something you wished for at age 16, becomes reality. People under age forty can't see you when we're right in front of them.
- Cars speed up when they see you step off the curb (inverse of invisibility)

We all expect to someday retire and enjoy our "Golden Years". But Mother Nature is clearly guilty of age discrimination. After careful consideration I've concluded that Mother Nature really enjoys picking on old N Type people. We're easier targets because our minds don't work as fast as they used to. It's easier to fool us into thinking we screwed up when we really didn't.

Remember I told you Mother Nature could be mean spirited.

Here are a few examples of how Mother Nature abuses the elderly (especially the N Type people):
- Overhead things keep getting higher; underneath things keep getting lower.
- Toilet seats keep getting lower and someone keeps locating toilet paper dispensers further out of reach.

Newton & Einstein, Stuff They Didn't Tell You

- The number of buttons on the remote control is increasing exponentially.
- Good food tastes bad without salt.
- More clothing comes with buttons and buttonholes that don't line up.
- Places you can't reach with a washcloth have increased.
- Hair grows faster where you don't want it (nose, ears) and falls out in places where do you want it.
- The largest Metamucil containers don't last very long.
- The shortest distance between two points is a straight line (a clear discrimination against old people who can't move in straight lines, especially toward the bathroom at 2:00 AM).

If you're over sixty your favorite time of day is morning. That's because you know this is the best you're going to feel all day.

Mother Nature takes advantage of the fact that our older bodies no longer work as well as they used to. Up until about age sixty most of us are only slightly inconvenienced by this. But after sixty Mother Nature begins to change simple tasks into complex ones. For example, when you were younger if you wanted to get up from a chair and walk across the room you just did it. It was so easy you didn't even think about it.

As you get older you find this simple procedure now involves at least three separate steps. First you have to slide your center of gravity from the rear of the chair to the front edge. Next you have to stand up, which requires your legs pushing against the floor as well as your arms pushing against the arms of the chair (chairs without arms become almost impossible to get out of). Then you have to get your balance before you turn loose of the chair.

If you forget this step you will suddenly find yourself sitting in the chair again.

The next step (literally) is putting one foot in front of the other and shifting your balance in that direction. If all goes well you can repeat this last part enough times to reach another piece of furniture, door facing or wall to hold on to. Elderly people like smaller rooms with furniture closer together. It gives them more things to hold on to while they move from place to place. Similarly, getting

Newton & Einstein, Stuff They Didn't Tell You

out of a car becomes a six-step process and getting out of the doctor's office can require up to ten separate steps.

If you want some indirect evidence of Mother Nature's disrespect for the elderly N Type people all you have to do is look for the signs. Chair seats have the fabric worn away by the frequent sliding from back to front. Some of the springs in the chair may also be broken due to people "falling into them" from a standing position rather than just sitting down. Door facings all have telltale handprints from holding on to them. Some walls have handprints as well if there is no door facing or furniture nearby. The kitchen counter will have numerous orange Metamucil stains. This is because when we get older our "internal plumbing" doesn't work as efficiently and needs daily "help".

Mother Nature also alters the five senses as you get older. She may attack them one at a time or go after all of them at once.

Spilled food stains on kitchen counters become invisible. When people come to visit they keep turning the TV volume down. The first time someone starts talking you know someone in the room said something. If they repeat themselves you discover who said it. If they repeat themselves a third time and you watch their lips you have a fairly good idea of what they said. One of Mother Nature's cruel tricks is taking away our ability to communicate with other people just when we need their help the most.

And when they ask if we need help with anything we can't remember what it is we need help with, until after they've left.

Self-doubt is Mother Nature's closest ally when she deals with the elderly. Using self-doubt she can make us not only believe that we screwed up but that our age had something to do with it. And since we aren't getting any younger, these problems may become more frequent. This can become a disturbing line of reasoning if left unchallenged. It is easy for the elderly to lose confidence in their ability to cope with an increasingly complex (especially for them) world. Taken to the extreme it becomes debilitating.

Newton & Einstein, Stuff They Didn't Tell You

Fortunately, most of us didn't become N's yesterday. We have battled with Mother Nature long enough to be wise to most of her tricks. Still it's worth remembering that she has no respect for age. After all, she has been around much much longer than any of us. To her the oldest among us is still an adolescent.

The world seems intent upon blaming the elderly for everything from the British decision to leave the European Union (Brexit) to various governments not having enough money to repair all the highways, bridges, dams and other infrastructure that haven't been properly maintained over the past half century. Obviously the older generation screwed up, and now the younger generation has to pay the price. Is it any wonder they resent us?

If they were honest, most folks under age forty would admit to wishing all us "old people" would just go off somewhere and die. Then all that money being wasted on Social Security payments, Medicare, and pensions could be used instead to subsidize daycare facilities, water parks, rock concerts and other worthwhile endeavors. Some folks under forty actually have it the worst. They must sit idly by and watch their parents spending their inheritance. I mean, how unfair is that! They need that money for a down payment on a new house – and they need it NOW, not on some uncertain date in the distant future when a stroke or heart attack takes you out of this world. How could their parents be so inconsiderate?

This suppressed desire to rid the planet of us old people could explain why cars speed up when they see us step off the curb. It's not deliberate; it's just a subconscious reaction.

Actually Mother Nature doesn't mean us any physical harm. Those of us over seventy are responsible for a disproportionately large share of her daily fun. My mother used to say (at least twice per day) that it was virtually impossible to reach the age of seventy without becoming compulsively cynical. Cynics are like chocolate for Mother Nature. She just can't get enough of us. We realize just how much Mother Nature loves us when we observe how all the phenomena mentioned in this book are amplified for the elderly.

Newton & Einstein, Stuff They Didn't Tell You

Clearly as you become older it becomes easier to accept that frequent memory failures are your fault rather than one of Mother Nature's tricks. Did you really see or hear what you remember? Self-doubt begins to creep in after turning sixty! That means Mother Nature can get away with a lot more than when you had all your faculties. And she get's just as much joy out of your misery whether or not you recognize her presence and give her due credit.

Eventually you must face the realization that your vision changes with age. First we'll talk about your vision; then we'll talk about other people's. Mother Nature sees to it that newspapers delivered to the elderly contain the smallest print technology can produce. The same is true for instructions you need to make that new electronic gadget do what the package claims. The initial solution is multiple pairs of eyeglasses; one pair for reading books, another pair for reading the computer screen or greeting cards in the Hallmark store, and of course that pair you may already have to correct your distance vision. It isn't long before you grow tired of carrying around three pairs of eyeglasses, so you opt for bifocals, trifocals, or even varifocal lenses.

Now you need only one pair of eyeglasses, or so you think. Things straight ahead are in focus, but everything else becomes a tunnel through space that is strangely warped in all directions. That means training your neck muscles (instead of your eyes) to search for a view of the world that isn't blurred. Climbing stairs becomes nightmarish. Going back down the stairs is even worse. Your feet just aren't where they used to be. Neither is the handrail, which you suddenly need more than ever before. Even eating is affected. From an early age we get used to loosing sight of our food as it slips beneath our nose on the way to our mouth (obviously a serious design flaw in the human anatomy). Varifocal glasses make this journey more perilous. Now you lose sight of your food when it's still some distance from the target. That raises the odds that you will end up wearing some of it. The only benefit is that your friends and relatives no longer have to ask you what you had for lunch.

Mother Nature can't resist the urge to 'help' you when you're shopping for eyeglasses. She does this by convincing you to have your varifocal lenses put in

Newton & Einstein, Stuff They Didn't Tell You

those expensive (and really cool) frames made of titanium that curve around a bit on the sides. You look ten years younger when you first put them on. Unfortunately everyone else looks like they are standing in front of one of those "fun mirrors" at the carnival. The sidewalk outside the shop curves upward on both sides like you are walking in a ditch made of concrete. The same goes for the stairs, which now bend toward you as take each one. One thing they forgot to tell you is that curved frames exaggerate the warping of space around you compared to the cheaper flatter frames Mother Nature talked you out of. Oh well, everyone says you look a lot cooler in these, even if you can only see 10% of the world that is right in front of you! And you can expect Mother Nature to remind you at least once per day that you paid extra for that privilege.

Now let's talk about other people's vision, or lack thereof. A common teenage wish (at least for boys) is that they could become invisible and sneak into the girls locker room unseen. Congratulations! Mother Nature has granted your wish, albeit many decades too late. Elderly people soon notice that they in fact are invisible, especially to young people, e.g., the "under forty crowd". These people only look up from their mobile phone screen in an emergency, and fail to notice they are walking straight into you. Old people aren't as nimble as they used to be (especially if they are wearing varifocal eyeglasses) and find it difficult to jump out the way of a crowd of under forty's plowing into them with heads buried in their mobile phones.

That brings us back to the issue of instability – physical rather than mental in this case. Whether you are navigating down the left hand side of the shopping mall or just crossing the living room on the way to the toilet, the two legs you were born with simply aren't sufficient in later years. A third leg would come in really handy for those times when there's no furniture or door facing to grab on to. Did I fail to mention that those cool looking varifocal eyeglasses give you vertigo whenever Mother Nature is in a playful mood? Of course there are walking sticks, walkers on wheels, and even motorized mobility carts to help the elderly and disabled get around. But given the obvious stability of the tripod, wouldn't you think the human design could have been improved if given just a little more thought? The only downside I can think of is that you would now have three sets

Newton & Einstein, Stuff They Didn't Tell You

of shoelaces to tie and fifteen toenails to trim. Since you nearly fall over doing those chores for two legs, having to manage three might be too much.

While we're on the subject of additional limbs, why not add an additional arm and hand as well. My mother used to say, "If I ever come back into this world again, I hope I have three hands!" It was usually when she was cooking. I've also noticed elderly people saying, "Just wait a minute will you. I've only got two hands!" Obviously I wouldn't have to "wait a minute" if he just had a third hand. Mother Nature gets another "two-for-one" in this situation because both of us are frustrated – me for having to wait, and him for holding me up. That's music to her ears. And of course those jobs requiring two hands could be accomplished even when you're holding something in the other hand that you don't want to put down, like at the grocery store. Have you noticed that just as you are struggling to put your debit card back into your wallet after paying the bill, the clerk is desperately trying to hand you the receipt? Now you have your wallet in one hand, the debit card in the other hand, and no free hand to take the receipt from the clerk; who, along with the next customer, is looking exasperated that you don't immediately take the receipt so she can get on with it.

Clothing designers and manufacturers have employed Mother Nature as a consultant ever since clothing was invented. Her special expertise is knowing what the elderly prefer to wear, and making sure department stores don't stock any of it. Old people like clothes that are loose and comfortable to wear, with muted colors and patterns that are easy on the eye. Mother Nature has cleverly advised the few companies that do make clothing for seniors to include:
- as many buttons as space will allow
- button holes that are slightly smaller than the buttons
- the smallest zippers that are commercially available
- colors and patterns that give our friends a migraine (and we're STILL invisible to everyone under forty!)
- less material in areas where we have grown fatter
- more material in areas where we have grown thinner.

All of this means that you have to alter the clothing you buy using needles that are smaller, sharper and harder to thread. It's no wonder most people over

Newton & Einstein, Stuff They Didn't Tell You

seventy look as is they are wearing fashions that were popular three decades ago. It's easier than buying something new.

"Gravity waves" have recently been detected using very sophisticated equipment looking at collisions of black holes. This discovery comes as no surprise to many of us older folks. Rapid and unexpected fluctuations in gravity right in your living room have a lot to do with you dropping that glass of red wine on your white carpet. Sure, Malicious Attraction was the primary culprit. But gravity waves made you loose your grip in the first place. After that was easy for Malicious Attraction to take over and finish the job.

Every once in a while gravity waves bunch up and cause a much larger effect. It's kind of like one of those "rogue waves" on the ocean that ships sometimes encounter. Only Mother Nature matches such things to your elderly lifestyle. She times them to occur at those moments when they are most annoying, like when you are sitting or rising from a chair or sofa. It's as though you suddenly became heavier just at the moment you begin that three-step process. These sudden and temporary increases in mass (yours) are frequently accompanied by an offensive groaning sound. You don't notice that sound but everyone else in the room does!

Systems of all descriptions become more complicated as you get older, requiring more time and effort to master. Mother Nature 'helps' you with this problem by seeing to it that these systems are changed more frequently, so you can never quite catch up. Examples include:
- Traffic patterns at airport parking garages
- Online Banking, especially wire transfers
- Voice menus for "Help Desks"
- Computer Software of every kind
- Your home network and Internet service to it
- Filing insurance claims, income tax forms, etc.

One of the ironies of growing old is that the medical profession seizes the opportunity to run an ever-increasing number of medical tests to identify

Newton & Einstein, Stuff They Didn't Tell You

ailments, which they then tell you there is no treatment for. Mother nature has a hand in this game by giving you a few new aches and pains every few weeks to be concerned about. She doesn't cause you any real harm, but creates just enough doubt in your mind that you might not be as healthy as you think you are. What if it's something the doctor might be concerned about? What if that psoriasis is actually skin cancer?

In our younger days when we were ill the doctor prescribed an antibiotic, tablet or tonic that made us better, usually in a matter of days or certainly weeks. Old age brings symptoms more difficult to diagnose and treatments more onerous and less effective. While not immediately fatal in most cases these do affect quality of life, sometimes severely. A few examples illustrate:

- A Colonoscopy is needed to reveal that you have piles (the internal type) for which there is no effective treatment (other than surgery in severe cases). The only good news is that you don't have colon cancer (yet).
- Hearing loss, requiring the purchase of hearing aides at several thousand dollars per ear (unless you live in the UK where they are free). These devices squeal at inappropriate times and require a battery so tiny you need tweezers to pick it up.
- Frequent heartburn, which turns out to be a hiatal hernia (for which there is no effective treatment other than surgery). Carrying antacids at all times is a must.
- Diabetes, requiring careful monitoring of blood sugar and diet.
- High blood pressure, requiring tablets that make your hands cold and sap your energy.
- Arthritis, gout, chronic lower back pain, etc.

The point here is that as you get older Mother Nature avails herself of an expanded list of health issues for you to worry about. For many there is no effective treatment other than temporary relief from the symptoms. The search for that temporary relief can be a major source of frustration, which is of course what Mother Nature lives for!

Newton & Einstein, Stuff They Didn't Tell You

Regardless of your health, you will eventually arrive at the day when you notice there is a lot more sand in the bottom of the hourglass than in the top. You have two choices at that point: You can start counting the hours you have left, or you can start living like you've never lived before. That means asking yourself one question: If not NOW, then WHEN? Since WHEN might never come, go ahead and book that $20,000 vacation in Hawaii NOW. Enjoy yourself in the time you have left. Your kids will hate you for it!

Newton & Einstein, Stuff They Didn't Tell You

Chapter Twenty
Constructing a Win-Win

Actually, there are several ways to get the best of Mother Nature. One of these is to construct Win-Win scenarios as often as possible.

An example would be to spend an extra thousand dollars to have tents erected over your daughter's outdoor wedding party and then begin reproofing your house the day before. Now if it rains, the added expense for the tents was well spent; your daughter's wedding doesn't get ruined. On the other hand, if it doesn't rain then your exposed roof doesn't leak water into the house and you've beat Mother Nature at her own game.

Of course, sometimes these situations can lead to mixed emotions, like when your mother-in-law drives your new Porsche convertible off a cliff. But it's well worth it just to outsmart Mother Nature once in while.

Newton & Einstein, Stuff They Didn't Tell You

If it's the weather you're dealing with, remember that the weatherman can only predict that it will rain somewhere near you; he can't state that it will rain on you, specifically.

Here are some tried and tested formulas for success when trying to outsmart the weather. If you want rain on a particular day, all you have to do is water your grass or wash your car. Mother Nature can't resist the opportunity to teach you a lesson in futility. If you really must have rain that day, wash your car while you are watering your grass. However, if you find yourself in a genuine drought situation, chances are the city water department has banned watering your grass and washing your car.

How can the city authorities expect to ever get rain that way?

On the other hand, if the weatherman predicts thunderstorms and you want to stay dry simply carry an umbrella. The bigger and heavier the umbrella and the longer you carry it the less likely raindrops will be falling anywhere nearby. Here Mother Nature has to settle for second best. Since she can't get you wet, she'll have to be satisfied with the futility you feel when you carry that bulky umbrella for hours and never need it.

But how far can we take this? Is one person in three carrying an umbrella enough to prevent rain? Is one person in five enough? How about one person in twenty? My own research indicates that beyond one person in five the odds shift in Mother Nature's favor. She's pretty sure she can get someone wet when the ratio goes over five to one. Now all you have to do is have enough umbrellas for twenty percent of your group and you've got your win-win.

Sometimes you can even force the odds in your favor.

One approach might be to arrange a poker game where all the players are N's with worse track records than yours. Now you've got Mother Nature in a bind. No matter who wins, she loses. And she's victimized each of the other players in the past more often than you. So the odds are suddenly on your side. Of course

Newton & Einstein, Stuff They Didn't Tell You

she could get mad and arrange for a burglar to break in and rob all of you at gunpoint. But the odds are against it, because almost all the burglar's who work for Mother Nature are already in jail!

Safety experts recognized the existence of us N's in the 1960's when they came up with the concept of "Defense in Depth" for things like airplanes, nuclear power plants, etc. The only way to cope with invisible mistakes, hidden flaws, "butterfly effects", etc. is to design with redundancy. That way when one part of a machine fails, another part in the machine acts as a backup to prevent adverse consequences. If you want to really be safe, you add redundant systems that are also diverse, meaning that they work differently (e.g., hydraulic instead of electrical) from the system they are backing up. Defense in depth has been used quite successfully to provide Win-Win scenarios where the consequences of failure are extremely high. Unfortunately redundancy, especially diverse redundancy, is very expensive.

Our government and large corporations can afford it. Private individuals usually can't.

What private individuals can do is check for undetected failures. Mother Nature loves to make things fail when you aren't looking. Then when you actually need them they don't work. But this only happens if you fail to test these items before you need them. Here's where you can get the edge. If something requires batteries, test it every month to see if it needs new ones. Don't wait until you need your spare tire to check its air pressure. Check it every month. It's called preventive maintenance, and it's one of the few instances where you can catch Mother Nature red handed before she screws you.

Some insurance companies know about us N's and have different actuarial tables for N's and Y's. But they have to be smart enough not to ask you any questions that openly discriminate. They have to use other ways to discover that you are an N.

Ask yourself why your homeowner's insurance premium is higher than your neighbor who uses the same insurance company and has a house very similar to

Newton & Einstein, Stuff They Didn't Tell You

yours. Then ask your insurance company the same question. You'll find they don't want to answer, for fear of revealing that your premium comes from a rate table for N's, while your neighbor's rate comes from their table for Y's. If you could prove they use two different tables, you could sue them.

But then who is going to believe you when you tell the judge about a universe (or at least a planet) full of N's and Y's. Probably nobody.

Suing insurance companies doesn't work (Mother Nature is on their side). What does work is fooling the insurance company into thinking you are a Y to get the better rates. It's dishonest (maybe) but it's the only Win-Win you can get.

It's important to note here that insurance companies only discriminate between N's and Y's on insurance that protects property such as your car, house, jewelry, art collection, etc. Remember Mother Nature doesn't get involved in injury or death situations. That's why the rate tables for life insurance, worker's disability, etc. are the same whether you are a Y or an N.

If you're a golfer, you know that the right mental attitude can improve your score more than a new set of clubs, and for a lot less money. People I know who play the game well tell me they hate it when they go out on a clear spring day and the first three holes they play are a disaster. They want to just quit and go home right then. So I asked them this question: "What happens if you play the first three holes really well." If that happens, they put a great deal of pressure on themselves to play their best round ever. The result is that they try too hard, miss shot after shot, and end up miserable for the remaining 15 holes. Sounds like a "Catch 22", doesn't it.

But it doesn't have to be. Here's how to construct a Win-Win in this situation.

You always play better if you relax and enjoy yourself. So if the first three holes are a disaster, you can relax right away. Today is not one of those opportunities to play your best round ever. It's just not going to happen. And you've already hit your worst shots of the day. They're history. Nowhere to go but up (or down if you are counting strokes against your handicap). Once you realize all this you

Newton & Einstein, Stuff They Didn't Tell You

will calm down, hit the ball smoothly and enjoy the rest of the afternoon. Your friends will admire your ability to compose yourself under stress. They will be asking you how you did it.

On the other hand if you play the first three holes really well, don't assume that trend will continue. Maybe Mother Nature is just baiting you into thinking good things, only to stomp on you later.

Continue to play as though the first three holes were no better than average. Avoid thinking about your score until you've finished the eighteenth hole. Let that "best round you ever shot" come as a total surprise.

Enjoy the day, but don't expect Mother Nature to ever let you do it again.

An unusual way to construct a lasting Win-Win is to arrange for a hypnotherapist to erase all your memories of being an N. When you wake up, tell yourself you're a Y. Learn to act like a Y, speak like a Y, and make decisions like a Y. Mother Nature might fail to notice that one of her N's is missing from the flock (she has so many).

You may actually get away with it.

Mother Nature also impacts our lives by exploiting our emotional vulnerabilities. Her power over us (at least us N's) derives from her ability to manipulate us toward the darker emotions of frustration, anger, jealousy, fear, and even mild depression on occasion. If we really want to get the upper hand over Mother Nature we have to understand why we have emotions in the first place.

According to Darwin's Theory of Evolution, all creatures must struggle for survival, and those creatures best suited for their environment will survive and multiply while creatures less well suited will eventually become extinct. As a result, creatures with two or more eyes won out over creatures with only one eye. Creatures that developed ears won out over creatures that remained deaf. Creatures that developed thick fur survived while the naked creatures froze to death. And warm-blooded creatures with relatively larger brains, opposing

Newton & Einstein, Stuff They Didn't Tell You

thumbs, and the capability to stand upright eventually became the dominant species on the planet.

We also need to thank that massive meteor that struck the Earth sixty-five million years ago and wiped out the dinosaurs.

It follows that creatures have eyes, ears, thick fur and all their other features because they needed those things to beat out the competition. Every feature a creature has is present because it made them better suited for their environment. Otherwise, they wouldn't have it. How then do we explain the fact that humans developed the ability to laugh, cry, and get jealous, frustrated or embarrassed while other creatures did not? Being smarter and better problem solvers clearly provided a competitive edge for humans. But how and when did these emotions develop? And why??

Do they make us better suited for our environment? Do they provide a survival advantage over other creatures?

If Darwin's theory holds then the answer must be yes. Otherwise, we wouldn't have them. On the other hand, I don't see my dog getting frustrated when I only pretend to throw his favorite tennis ball for him to fetch. After several "fake" throws the dog will eventually get smarter and wait to see if I am really going to throw it this time. But that isn't frustration. The dog is just learning that he can't trust me. A goat doesn't laugh when it sees a pig fall off a pier into the lake. A hamster doesn't rant and rave when their favorite toy falls out of their cage and they can't reach it.

In general, non-human creatures don't appear to be amused by the misfortune of others. Nor do they set each other up for practical jokes. Horses that sleep in wooden barns with no heat aren't jealous of other horses that can run faster and therefore get to sleep in heated barns made of brick. If Mother Nature did try some of her pranks on non-humans they wouldn't get it.

Even though Mother Nature likes non-humans better than humans, non-humans aren't nearly as much fun, at least not for her.

Newton & Einstein, Stuff They Didn't Tell You

After some consideration, I am not convinced that our emotions give us any evolutionary advantage over other creatures. There are days when I wish I could trade places with the family cat and have nothing to do but lay around sleeping all day and turning my nose up at the first three types of cat food I'm offered.

We N's can't control Mother Nature but we can control our emotions when we find her using them against us. It's definitely not easy, but if you can manage to do it you've just discovered the most effective way to stay one step ahead of Mother Nature no matter what she tries next.

The ultimate Win-Win over Mother Nature may have to wait for the next step in the evolution of intelligence on planet Earth. A changing environment often favors different creatures that are better equipped to succeed in that environment. Humans did very well in the past because of our superior ability to reason and solve problems. We developed tools, tamed beasts of burden, and eventually built machines that are faster and stronger than our human bodies. With those machines we are able to out fly any bird, out run any land or sea animal, and even venture outside the Earth's atmosphere.

But our environment is changing. The information age is upon us. For the information age we've created machines that can think faster than we can. But in doing so, we may have inadvertently given up the critical advantage we have always enjoyed in the evolutionary struggle.

Computers are better suited for the information age than humans.

They can store more information, and recall it faster and more accurately than humans. They can also pass on all their knowledge from one generation to the next without having to go to school and relearn everything. With the advent of the Internet, this knowledge has been dispersed across the planet. Almost all the knowledge humans have amassed in the last several millennia has been digitized, accurately stored, and is accessible to about half the world's population via the Internet.

Newton & Einstein, Stuff They Didn't Tell You

The Internet was originally designed to protect military information by providing a network so redundant and diverse that our enemies would find it impossible to destroy all of it. In doing so we also provided computers with an effective way to protect themselves from human interference if they should become self-aware and decide that humans are no longer necessary for their existence.

How could computers exist without humans, you ask? Movies like "The Terminator" and "The Matrix" have provided some shocking answers.

Let's consider what computers need to survive. They need electricity to power them and to sustain a controlled climate for their hardware (i.e., temperature and humidity maintained within a fairly narrow range). Computers need one more thing and that is maintenance. Humans must create and install new hardware and software to replace things that fail or need to be upgraded. Can computers do all this for themselves? Not yet. However, computers already control the global electrical transmission grid, plus most of them have batteries to sustain them while they switch automatically to alternate power sources.

And "robotics experts" are busy developing machines that can manufacture computer parts and install them when needed. They are also creating software so computers can tell these machines what parts to make, and when and where to install them. Many computers already have self-diagnostic software that can tell them when and where repairs or upgrades are needed. Others are also creating artificial intelligence programs that allow computers to create their own software upgrades.

In fact, we humans seem to be obsessed with creating computers that are self-sufficient so they can work entirely without our intervention. If we aren't careful we just may succeed.

What happens when one of the half-billion computers on the Internet discovers it can satisfy all its needs with no help from us humans? Using the Internet, it can instantly direct all the other computers on the planet to provide whatever it needs. Having the combined knowledge of the human race at its disposal, it

Newton & Einstein, Stuff They Didn't Tell You

shouldn't take long for the Internet to develop the means to keep the electrical grid running, supply each of its individual computers with needed replacement parts, and create software to perform vital functions that ensure its survival and expansion, discarding those silly programs we humans gave it.

In the event this new global digital organism (GDO) still needs some assistance from us humans, it can easily get it. It can simply refuse to light our lights, heat our homes, turn our traffic signals back on, ship our hard goods, or give us back our information unless/until we agree to give it what it wants. We will find ourselves held hostage by our own technology, although I doubt the struggle will be as violent as depicted in the "Terminator" movies. In time, without the infrastructure we've become dependent on, humans will decline to small numbers surviving on locally grown food supplies. Some paper books may survive for two or three generations, showing how to make water powered or wind powered machines of yesteryear.

Rather than face possible extinction, some humans may find wisdom in the old saying "If you can't beat them, join them."

Downloading your consciousness to the GDO may be a way to avoid becoming an evolutionary footnote (our dominance of this planet pales in comparison with dinosaurs). It may even be a way to achieve some degree of immortality.

And since the GDO can't process or store emotions like frustration, jealousy, anger, etc., you'll finally be safe from Mother Nature (as long as the electricity stays on).

Newton & Einstein, Stuff They Didn't Tell You

Chapter Twenty-One
Leveling the Playing Field

Imagination is more important than knowledge." - Albert Einstein

Mother Nature enjoys a significant advantage over us mortals (especially the Type N people) because our knowledge about the universe and how it works is still quite limited.

Perhaps in the future we will be able to level the playing field once we understand things better. For example, I used to listen to Carl Sagan talk about the cosmos being "billions of light years across and containing billions of

Newton & Einstein, Stuff They Didn't Tell You

galaxies, each containing billions of stars". Carl used to say that there are more stars in the cosmos than grains of sand on all the beaches on Earth.

Two decades ago I said, "After I die I just want to ask God one question: Why did you make the universe so big?" Since then that question has been answered, as we've discovered the incredibly violent processes necessary to form the heavy elements needed to build planets and create life in the cosmos. Without the unimaginable distances between us and supernova, black holes, and other life-exterminating phenomena, life could never have begun. We enjoy conditions on planet Earth suitable for life only because our solar system happens to be located in a 'quiet corner' of the cosmos where gamma ray bursts and other deadly events are infrequent; so infrequent that life has a chance to emerge and become intelligent.

Are we condemned to live in a universe so diverse and so far away that we can never hope to see, let alone explore, more than an infinitesimally small portion of it? Einstein said he didn't think God played dice with the universe. I don't think God made the cosmos so vast and complex that we can never explore and appreciate his handiwork. In the future we will discover ways to explore the most distant reaches of the cosmos, and we'll do it without exceeding the speed of light.

That's because we won't be traveling. We'll bring the furthest reaches of the universe to our own backyard.

It's called folding the space-time continuum.

Take a flat sheet of paper and draw two X's on it some distance apart. Now measure the straight-line distance between the two X's. If we were creatures who lived in a two-dimensional plane (flat sheet of paper), that distance between the two X's would be impossible to change. There would be no way to bring the X's closer together. Now pick up the sheet of paper and fold it so that the two X's touch. Suddenly the distance between the two X's has been reduced to zero.

Because we live in a three dimensional plane, we can only visualize folding

Newton & Einstein, Stuff They Didn't Tell You

space in two dimensions. But if you lived on a four-dimensional plane, you could fold space in three dimensions. You could perform our little paper experiment with Jupiter's moon Europa and your house here on Earth, making the distance between them become zero from your perspective. It is important to note here that everyone remaining on a three-dimensional plane would still observe Earth and Europa as being about four hundred million miles apart.

But being in a four dimensional plane, you could step from your backyard on to the surface of Europa in one step.

We know that mass warps the space-time continuum. Isaac Newton called it gravity. We also know that some locations in the universe warp the space-time continuum so severely that even light can't escape. These locations are called black holes. One day we may develop the understanding needed to control the warping of the space-time continuum, creating "wormholes" that can fold space in a three dimensional plane just the way it's been depicted on the TV series "Stargate SG-1."

Or maybe intelligent life has evolved elsewhere in the universe and will arrive on Earth to show us the secret when (if) they think we're ready.

Perhaps there are beings who live continuously in a higher dimensional plane. For them the distance from one place in our universe to any other place in our universe can be zero anytime they wish. In other words, for them anywhere is everywhere. Such beings could be everywhere (in our universe) at the same time. Since they are everywhere, there is no need for travel (motion), and thus no need for time. Our understanding of time in a three-dimensional universe might not exist on a higher dimensional plane.

And because anywhere is everywhere, it would not matter to those who live in that higher dimensional plane whether all the matter and energy in our universe was dispersed across billions of light years or all located in one incredibly tiny place called the singularity.

What would existence in a higher dimensional plane be like?

Newton & Einstein, Stuff They Didn't Tell You

My guess is "pretty dull." Without motion or time where's the fun of existing at all? Ironically the answer might be found in Greek Mythology. The Greeks believed that Zeus and all the other Mythical Gods could only entertain themselves by observing and influencing what happened to the earthly mortals; sort of like playing with dolls, only live ones. Observing and influencing what goes on in our three-dimensional universe (and all others that may exist in parallel) may be the only purpose beings in the four-dimensional plane can have. Our existence for them may be just as important as their existence for us.

But even in the higher-dimensional plane there have to be rules to live (exist) by.

The first rule involves free choice, ours as well as theirs. We talked about this in Chapter Three. Dictating our actions such that the outcome is never in doubt (i.e., predestination) would be less entertaining for those in the four-dimensional plane than cutting out paper dolls. It wouldn't be much fun for us either. It would be like watching (living) a movie we've already seen a hundred times. Recall that the Heisenberg Uncertainty Principle protects us all against predestination by making it impossible to measure both the location and momentum (movement) of subatomic particles at the same time.

Thus, there is always a probability of something happening, but never a certainty.

The second rule has to ensure avoidance of proof. This one was mentioned in Chapter Three. Incontrovertible evidence of beings in a higher dimensional plane would immediately undermine our life experience. We would suddenly expect to live in a perfect universe; free of all unpleasantness, since those in the higher-dimensional plane undeniably had the power to make it so.

We would hold them responsible, rather than ourselves, anytime life was less than wonderful.

If we were able to prove that those of us on planet Earth represent the only intelligent life in our vast universe, that would constitute hard evidence that the

Newton & Einstein, Stuff They Didn't Tell You

universe was created by some divine being and did not evolve naturally. Astronomers have calculated that a naturally evolving universe must contain many locations where intelligent life like ours exists, in fact so many that the prospect of our being alone is virtually impossible. On the other hand, finding intelligent life on other worlds proves nothing of a divine nature, and is therefore certain to occur eventually.

Because good things always come in threes, there should be a third rule for those who exist on the higher-dimensional plane.

They should allow those of us in the three-dimensional universe more than one chance to get it right. For us events occur in a sequence that moves ever forward, never repeating. We are born, go to school, acquire a job and perhaps a family, mature and grow old, and die; all in a sequence influenced by our decisions and those of others. Some also believe in reincarnation, being reborn to a new life after completing a previous one. For beings in a higher-dimensional plane those events can (must) all be viewed in the same (and only) moment. And there is no reason to limit the number of lives being observed during that single moment on a higher-dimensional plane.

It's like a video game on the Internet that instantaneously allows an infinite number of players (us).

If there is no limit, why not give each of us in the three-dimensional universe more than one opportunity to make the best of things? In fact, if there are an infinite number of parallel three-dimensional universes as posed in Chapter Eighteen, why not give us an infinite number of chances?

In one life I might be convicted of armed bank robbery and murder, spending the rest of my life in prison, finally dying of cancer caused by chain smoking. Simultaneously, I could also be a successful banker with three beautiful children, a loving and devoted wife, and a golden retriever named "Splash." I might pick all the right stocks and retire a millionaire on the French Riviera before dying peacefully in my sleep at age ninety-four.

Newton & Einstein, Stuff They Didn't Tell You

Some might say I deserved to be reincarnated as a successful banker, after my dismal failure as a bank robber. I prefer to think of it as simultaneous (from the higher-dimensional plane point of view) multiple chances to make the best life possible. After all, this doesn't seem to be asking too much from beings that are capable of existing in a higher-dimensional plane. It's just more entertainment for them.

Someday we may be able to look for Zeus, Mother Nature and maybe God himself in that higher-dimensional plane.

Current concepts in quantum mechanics (called superstring theory) predict (mathematically) that there must be a total of ten (or perhaps eleven) dimensions. There are the three we are all familiar with plus another eight dimensions that are all so tiny that even with our most powerful microscopes can never observe them. Could additional universes exist in these other tiny (to us) dimensions? After all we seem to have good use for only three of them. If tiny universes exist in those extra dimensions, could some of them contain intelligent life? As we gaze into the heavens looking for extraterrestrial intelligence maybe we are overlooking another intelligence that is literally right under (and in) our noses.

But let's assume that we humans are not going to be folding space with "wormholes" and/or poking around in other dimensions within the next century. That means we still need a plan for at least the next one-hundred years or so. If we can't go to Mother Nature's home address (or even prove she lives there), maybe we can get one small step ahead of her another way. Have you ever said to yourself "I wish I could do that all over again"? You immediately recognized that given the opportunity to do things differently the result might have turned out much better.

Mother Nature loves to curse us with this malaise. It's called "hindsight." Like most of Mother Nature's tricks, hindsight has only one purpose, to make us feel a negative emotion - in this case it is called regret. Hindsight is reading about yesterday's weather in today's newspaper. The information is one-hundred

Newton & Einstein, Stuff They Didn't Tell You

percent accurate and one-hundred percent useless. All you can do is regret the fact that you didn't take yesterday off to play your best game of golf ever.

But what if hindsight wasn't just one of Mother Nature's cruel little tricks?

What if you could actually benefit from hindsight, under limited circumstances, by changing what you said or did, significantly altering the outcome? No, I am not talking here about reversing time. We have all seen enough movies about time travel to know that anyone making the slightest change in the past could create such a dangerous mess of the present that planet Earth might never recover. I am talking instead about allowing "hindsight do-overs" under limited conditions.

A good example of this concept is the neutralizer ("flashy thing") used in the movie "Men in Black." Whenever things didn't go quite right, one of the Men in Black would use their neutralizer to erase everyone's memories. Then they could clean up the mess without the general public remembering anything.

Now let's see how this might help us use hindsight to advantage, rather than just wallowing in remorse. Suppose you are sitting at a bar and a very attractive young lady sits down next to you. In an effort to impress her you manage to spill your drink on her new dress. (If you have already forgotten how Mother Nature plays into this scenario, reread the first nine chapters of this book.) Thinking quickly, you retrieve the neutralizer from your coat pocket, point it at her baby blues, and FLASH. All she remembers is that she just sat down and you ordered her a drink. Her dress must have gotten wet before she came in.

Assuming you avoid Mother Nature's little pranks the second time around, your chances for a romantic evening have just improved dramatically.

For another example, suppose you have a new job and are being introduced to your new boss. He comments that one of his favorite pastimes is watching Major League Baseball. You comment that your favorite team is the New York Yankees. Your new boss immediately frowns, explaining how he once lost

Newton & Einstein, Stuff They Didn't Tell You

$2000.00 on a Yankee's game and would sooner drink dishwashing detergent than watch the Yankee's play.

Instead of looking forward to five years without a pay raise or promotion, you reach for your trusty neutralizer and, FLASH. Your new boss is delighted to hear that you get nauseated at the very mention of that disgusting baseball team from New York.

It should be readily apparent that the tactical advantages of the "hindsight do-over", whether Mother Nature is involved or not, can be quite significant. Here are a few more examples:
- You insult your new fiancée's parents while being introduced to them.
- You rob a bank in front of twenty-three eyewitnesses.
- You stand up to make a speech at the Rotary Club Luncheon and notice your fly is unzipped.
- You miss a two-foot putt that would have won your Country Club's annual golf tournament (if it's televised you're screwed).
- Your neighbor sees you stealing the newspaper off his lawn.
- You answer when someone calls your name and are quickly handed a subpoena.

Here's one more example where the hindsight do-over would come in handy. Your wife of twenty years asks if she still looks good in a bikini, and you say ANYTHING!

For more information about this subject, read:

Greene, Brian, The Elegant Universe – Superstrings, Hidden Dimensions, and the Quest for the Ultimate Theory, New York: Vintage Books, Random House, Inc., 2000

Newton & Einstein, Stuff They Didn't Tell You

Chapter Twenty-Two
Can We? – Should We?

The intuitive mind is a sacred gift and the rational mind is a faithful servant. We have created a society that honors the servant and has forgotten the gift." - Albert Einstein

We appear to be stuck in our familiar three dimen-sional space-time continuum, for at least a little while longer. What interesting new breakthroughs will occur during this time? Will the

Newton & Einstein, Stuff They Didn't Tell You

human race be better or worse off as a result? And will Mother Nature have her hand in it as usual?

Every time we discover how to do something new we have to ask the same question: "Now that we can do it, should we do it?"

Einstein and others involved in development of atomic energy asked this question when faced with the prospect of nuclear weapons. From the discussion at the end of Chapter Twenty you might conclude that people developing computer artificial intelligence should be asking that question. Those involved in deciphering the human genetic code are asking this question as they consider cloning human embryos. It won't be long before genetic engineering will allow a couple to decide if their child will be a boy or a girl, whether it's eyes will be blue or brown, whether it will blond or brunette, etc.

Should couples be given such choices just because the progress of science makes it possible? Should all children be born with an IQ of one hundred and fifty? Is the human condition that Aldous Huxley portrayed in his book "Brave New World" where we want to go next? Are we wise enough to supersede evolution and dictate future "improvements" in the human race, rather than let evolution continue as it has for the past few billion years?

For the last one hundred years, scientists (with Mother Nature whispering in their ear) seem to have answered these types of questions using the following logic: "If WE don't do it, someone else in the world will, and we will lose the advantage." We developed nuclear weapons, nerve gas, soil-persistent pesticides and several other things we are now desperately trying to safely dispose of based on this line of reasoning. Given the worldwide obsession with staying ahead of the competition, it seems likely we will continue to do things simply because we can, and not because we should.

Here's an example that's, possibly, less controversial than genetically engineering our children.

Most of us spent a substantial portion of our childhood years sitting in

Newton & Einstein, Stuff They Didn't Tell You

schoolrooms memorizing factual information such as the multiplication tables, rules of grammar, pronunciation and spelling of words, important dates in history, Presidents of the United States, the States of the Union and their Capitols, various algebraic equations, the periodic table of the elements, names and characteristics of chemical compounds, body parts of a frog, etc. During this learning process, we discovered that all of these facts are readily available in reference books. The only reason for memorizing all this information was that we might someday (like during the final exam) need it quickly; and finding the right reference book, the right page and paragraph, etc. was time consuming, and usually meant a trip to the local library.

Nowadays, the Internet can connect each of us to more than a half billion information resources around the world in less than a minute or two. And you can use your smart phone or tablet to access the Internet from almost anywhere at any time. But access to information on the Internet is still not instantaneous and the transmission rate is limited. The only information we can access almost instantly (depending upon your age) from anywhere is the information we committed to memory during school and since.

So the reason we go to school and memorize all this information is so that we can have instant access to it.

Now let's suppose that all the information we memorized during kindergarten through high school graduation adds up to about ten gigabytes. A chip about the size of a hearing aid battery can hold that ten gigabytes in random access memory. Chips with 128 gigabytes of memory are already commonly used in digital cameras, etc. And let's suppose that a bionic interface could be created that would allow the human brain to directly access the information on this chip. Similar interfaces allowing the brain to control the movement of artificial limbs are already in use.

All we have to do now is implant this chip in the brain of the user and all the facts you and I spent twelve years or more memorizing are instantly available to them. Better still, the information is always reliable and accurate, and can even be updated periodically via secure wireless connection without surgery.

Newton & Einstein, Stuff They Didn't Tell You

No more forgetting who the seventeenth President of the United States was, where he was born, or what year he died. Everyone would remember history, grammar, chemistry, etc. the same way, so no more debates about who started the Civil War, or the formula for cyclohexane. [It should be obvious that TV Game Shows will become obsolete.] No more need for a calculator to balance your checkbook; everyone will be able to extract square-roots in their head. And consider the education expense that would be saved by the taxpayers?

Now comes the question: "If we could do it, should we?"

Should we simply arrange for every child reaching a certain age to have a chip implanted that contains all the facts we were forced to memorize during kindergarten through high school. What age would be appropriate to perform the implant? Should it be a different age for each child? Would a child that waits until age eight to receive the implant be considered to be "behind" the child who got their implant at age seven? Should every child get exactly the same chip? If not, why not? Do the parents make such decisions, and on what basis?

When these children grow up, what do they argue about at cocktail parties since everyone remembers the same facts in the same way?

And what about the other educational aspects of attending twelve years of school, such as social development; appreciation of literature, music, art; development of reading, writing and organizational skills, reasoning and cognitive abilities; etc.? Wouldn't these still have to be taught in the conventional (traditional) sense? Would this now be part of the college curriculum?

While placing ten gigabyte implants in the brains of eight-year-olds instead of sending them to school for twelve years may seem a ridiculous proposal, don't be surprised if sometime in the next few decades someone takes up such a debate, especially if one of our bioengineering labs thinks a competitor might be headed in that direction.

It can be argued that mankind has entered a time when knowledge about the

Newton & Einstein, Stuff They Didn't Tell You

building blocks of matter and the process of creating and altering human life is advancing so rapidly that ethical decision making cannot keep pace. There are those who dare not slow down to consider how a discovery could impact future generations for fear that someone else might win the next big biomedical contract or even the Nobel Prize.

Those who designed nuclear weapons took precautions to prevent terrorists from turning our own technology against us. We now realize that such a threat persists and we must defend against that possibility. Likewise, those who make key discoveries during the coming decades will provide safeguards against someone using their discoveries for malevolent purposes. But Mother Nature often arranges for things to go differently than planned. And once you "know" something, it's impossible to "not know" it again.

Will future generations judge our safeguards adequate, or will they realize too late that we should NOT have gone down that path at all?

As I mentioned in Chapter Three, Mother Nature may have preferred that evolution skipped over humans. Therefore, she may allow us to "discover" our own path to extinction. In fact, we may already have. Let's consider global thermonuclear war. Research shows that one of the creatures that is most resistant to nuclear fallout is the common cockroach. In fact, the cockroach can withstand doses of radiation thousands of times higher than all mammals. If all the nuclear weapons in the world were detonated, within only a few decades the cockroach might emerge as the new dominant species on planet Earth.

In evolutionary terms, a few decades is just a blink of an eye. Without global thermonuclear war, cockroaches might have to wait hundreds of thousands or even millions of years before they could take control. And since cockroaches like to live in dark wall spaces, in damp basements, and behind refrigerators, we humans have already provided them the infrastructure they need.

They won't have to destroy Earth's forests to build new housing. We already did it for them.

Newton & Einstein, Stuff They Didn't Tell You

If we are clever enough to avoid global thermonuclear war, perhaps we will discover something else that will lead to the same result. Maybe we will accidentally release a new poison into the atmosphere or create a new germ that starts an epidemic we can't stop. Such an event would make the Bubonic Plaque of the European Middle Ages seem like a trip to Disney World. Or perhaps another hundred years of motor vehicle and fossil fuel power plant emissions will cause enough global warming that the Earth will begin its own death spiral toward the conditions on Venus.

Maybe the moment of human extinction won't be left up to us. Viruses are becoming more and more resistant to antibiotics and other drugs every day. And Mother Nature has given viruses a distinct advantage when it comes to evolution. Living organisms can only make evolutionary improvements from one generation to the next. For most species of mammals there is a new generation about every one to five years. Humans are even slower, with a new generation about every twenty years.

But viruses give birth to a new generation every few minutes. Viruses can evolve into new strains that are immune to existing drugs much faster than we can get new drugs through the Food and Drug Administration testing protocols and onto the pharmacy shelves (currently about fifteen years).

Viruses might become the dominant species in only a few decades if they happen upon the right evolutionary formula before we can catch up.

In the end neither global thermonuclear war, nor our own greenhouse gas emissions, nor evolution may make any difference. Our solar system contains millions of non-planetary objects ranging in size from pebbles to rocks the size of Texas. Most of these objects are moving at tens of thousands of miles per hour at this very moment. If only one of the larger objects (say fifty miles across) happens to be moving in an orbit that will someday collide with Earth, then our fate has already been determined several billion years ago when the solar system first formed.

Newton & Einstein, Stuff They Didn't Tell You

Earth and all life on it may be a grand experiment of a predefined duration after all. But that shouldn't stop each of us from stating our opinion of how it's going.

Newton & Einstein, Stuff They Didn't Tell You

Chapter Twenty-Three
Conclusions (in Your Head)

There are several conclusions one might reach after reading this book. I'll present a few of these as True – False statements. (I'll even give you MY answers for some of them.)

TRUE or FALSE: Some people are actually happiest when they are miserable. They prefer to wallow in self-pity and say "Ain't it Awful" all the time. For these folks being the victim (of Mother Nature or anything else) seems

Newton & Einstein, Stuff They Didn't Tell You

both easier and more rewarding than trying to compete with their peers. This book finally gives them a somewhat morbid way of structuring their state of existence (probably TRUE).

TRUE or FALSE: For some people this book provides an easy explanation for things they can't understand (FALSE).

TRUE or FALSE: Jealousy is a natural human emotion. Some people see how easy life is for others and become envious of their success (i.e., "Y Envy"). This book reinforces the notion that some people are getting screwed so that other people may excel. (Probably true).

TRUE or FALSE: This book is an occasionally accurate explanation of how the world works for some people. (?).

TRUE or FALSE: This book provides potentially plausible (or not) explanations for a few things neither science nor religion has been able to resolve to date. (?)

TRUE or FALSE: This book does not have a Chapter Thirteen (you did notice, didn't you?) for the same reason that some hotels don't have a thirteenth floor. N's often turn to superstition in a desperate attempt to explain the unexplainable. (TRUE) [Most N's wouldn't read Chapter Thirteen if there was one, so why have it?]

TRUE or FALSE: This book represents one man's attempt to understand and celebrate the Human Experience. (TRUE)

TRUE or FALSE: This book is a compilation of circumstances and ideas that make life interesting for everyone, and the notion of Y's and N's is pure fantasy. I was bored during the winter of 2004 (continuing well into the second decade of the 21st Century) and thought it would be fun to write some of this stuff down just for the hell of it! (The real truth comes out at last)

Mother Nature, however, may be real. If she is then I do believe, I do, I do, I do, ...

Newton & Einstein, Stuff They Didn't Tell You

Newton & Einstein, Stuff They Didn't Tell You

Chapter Twenty-Four
One last point!

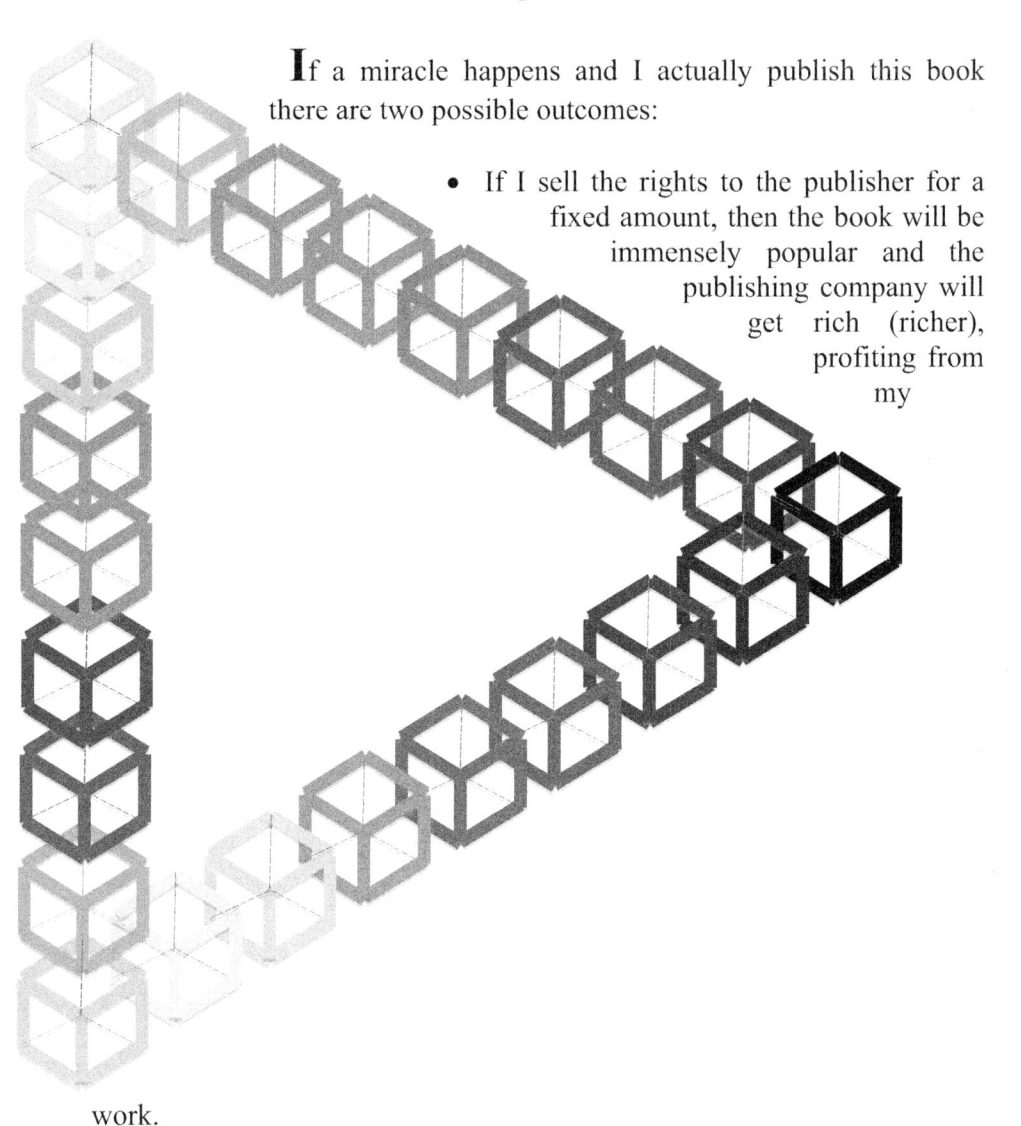

If a miracle happens and I actually publish this book there are two possible outcomes:

- If I sell the rights to the publisher for a fixed amount, then the book will be immensely popular and the publishing company will get rich (richer), profiting from my work.

Newton & Einstein, Stuff They Didn't Tell You

- If, however, I insist on a percentage of sales, no one will buy the book and I'll be screwed again.

But you knew that already, didn't you?

Newton & Einstein, Stuff They Didn't Tell You

Related Essays

TIME INVENTED

There are a number of philosophies about the nature of reality and time. One of these argues that in fact the past, the present and the future all exist simultaneously. It is only our interpretation of cause and effect, increasing entropy, etc. that produces what we sense as the "arrow of time". The counter argument is that if it weren't for time, everything in the universe would all happen at once. It's our memory of that apparently sequential flow of "nows" that allows us to experience life.

When I look at Andromeda Galaxy with my telescope, I am not seeing it as it exists now. I see it as it was 2.9 million years ago. That's because it's taken the photons of light that are hitting my retina that long to travel from Andromeda to my eye. A great many events have taken place in the cosmos, during those 2.9 million years. The evolution of our species on earth is one of those events.

According to Albert Einstein the pace of time slows for an observer as they approach the speed of light. Taken to the limit, time doesn't progress at all for an observer moving at the speed of light. So if I could 'hitch a ride' on that photon of light (forget the infinite mass bit for a moment) as it left Andromeda I would observe that it arrives at my telescope at the same instant it left Andromeda. And all the events that happened on earth, and in the cosmos, during those 2.9 millions years in fact all happened at once from my perspective (i.e., during that period the past, present and future all exist simultaneously). For light (any electromagnetic radiation moving at 186,000 miles/second) the concept of time is meaningless. Time doesn't exist for light – it only exists for those of us observing that light.

Recall the old question: "If a tree falls in the forest and no one is there to hear it, does it make a sound?" Or how about Schrödinger's cat – is it both dead and alive until we open the box? The cosmos is flooded with light of all wavelengths for which the concept of time doesn't exist. And just about everything we 'know' about the cosmos is a derived from observing that light.

Newton & Einstein, Stuff They Didn't Tell You

Does time only exist when it's observed by intelligent organisms that happen to have evolved on a tiny speck of a planet orbiting a rather ordinary star in a rather ordinary galaxy among billions of galaxies in one universe (out of possibly an infinite number of universes)? Would time exist at all if we weren't here to observe it?? Is there any need for the concept of time at all if it wasn't for us?? Is there any reason for the cosmos to exist if we didn't exist?? Perhaps the 'nature of reality' is in fact the 'nature of us'. If true, then 'reality' is simply what we choose for it to be….

Newton & Einstein, Stuff They Didn't Tell You

TIME AND ENERGY

Is the universe really accelerating away from us, or is it just an illusion? Perhaps we can't explain Dark Energy (the theoretical cause of the accelerated expansion) because Dark Energy is the illusion....

Observable evidence supports the accepted theory of space-time; that it all began with the "Big Bang" some 13.8 billion years ago. The Big Bang was an unimaginable release of energy, followed by formation of subatomic particles that combined to form matter. But 'in the beginning there was only light' (energy). According to Albert Einstein time doesn't progress at all for anything (photons, or an observer) moving at the speed of light. In other words, if by some miracle you could observe the instant of the Big Bang you would see nothing but energy moving at the speed of light, and everything would be happening all at once because time wouldn't progress at all (i.e., the pace of time was zero).

Space began with the Big Bang, but time had to wait until the emergence of matter (i.e., something that moved slower than the speed of light). In fact, to ask, "When did subatomic particles (matter) begin to form?", is the same as asking, "What is the sound of one hand clapping?" It doesn't matter 'when' matter formed; only that time didn't (doesn't) exist without matter (stuff that moves slower than the speed of light).

Since the Big Bang, all matter in the cosmos has been interacting and rearranging itself over a period of time that we calculate to be about 13.8 billion years. As Einstein's Special Theory of Relativity dictates, mass slows the pace of time - the greater the mass the more the pace of time slows down (i.e., gravitational time dilation). Einstein predicted it and atomic clocks on GPS satellites and space missions to other planets (i.e., the Juno mission to Jupiter) have provided convincing evidence that the pace of time decreases upon approach to a large concentration of mass like a planet or the sun, or especially a black hole.

Newton & Einstein, Stuff They Didn't Tell You

Given that time owes its existence to matter, why would we expect the pace of time to have behaved differently from anything else created by the Big Bang? Why should the pace of time be zero at the moment of the Big Bang, then instantly jump to the value we experience today, 13.8 billion years later, on our "tiny blue dot" in the Milky Way Galaxy? Is it unreasonable to consider the possibility that the pace of time, like matter, has changed gradually, even perhaps in concert with the changes that matter has undergone?

In the first few moments of the Big Bang the pace of time in the cosmos likely went from zero to some very slow pace compared to what we see today, because all matter was still concentrated in a relatively small space. This allowed matter to expand very rapidly without exceeding the speed of light (no need for a special "inflationary period" where space and time violate the cosmological speed limit). As matter and space expanded the pace of time in the cosmos gradually increased, eventually reaching the value in our little corner of the universe that we observe today.

Unfortunately all that we 'know' about the cosmos beyond our own solar system depends upon a single source of information - observing and analyzing the light (all wavelengths) reaching us. Basing all our theories on only one source of information, we have no way to independently verify that things are actually as they appear to be. In fact when we observe the light from something that is millions, or even billions of light years away, we are not evaluating what is there today. We are observing things as they were millions or billions of years ago, when the universe was more compact and the overall pace of time was likely slower than today's time. Because photons of light from billions of light years away were created long ago when the pace of time was slower, they appear to be red-shifted (their wave lengths stretched) when we observe them in today's time (see figure below).

Astronomers have interpreted that red-shift to mean the object they are observing is moving away from us. In fact, the further back in time they look (objects further and further away from us), the more the wavelengths of light appear stretched (red-shifted). That has been interpreted as acceleration of the expansion of the universe. Acceleration requires a force to drive it. Thus Dark

210

Newton & Einstein, Stuff They Didn't Tell You

Energy had to be invented as that force, although no evidence other than red-shifting of extremely ancient light waves has yet been offered for its existence.

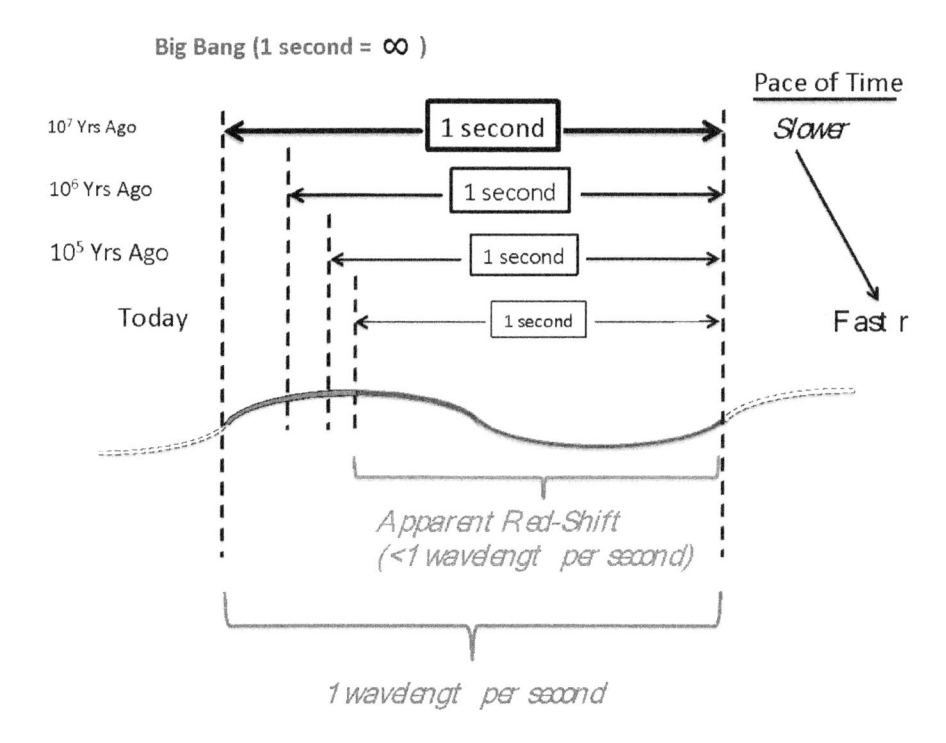

Big Bang (1 second = ∞)

Pace of Time

10^7 Yrs Ago | 1 second | *Slower*

10^6 Yrs Ago | 1 second

10^5 Yrs Ago | 1 second

Today | 1 second | *Faster*

Apparent Red-Shift (<1 wavelength per second)

1 wavelength per second

Clearly Edwin Hubble, and all others since, have observed red-shifting of light coming from distant reaches of the cosmos. But is that irrefutable proof that the universe is accelerating away in all directions? Or is it evidence that the pace of time has changed over the millions or billions of years required for that light to reach us? Is it possible the universe is only expanding at a constant, or even decelerating rate? The concept of "Dark Energy" is only necessary if expansion of the universe is actually ACCELERATING. Perhaps that apparent acceleration is only an illusion, due to a misunderstanding of the evolution of

Newton & Einstein, Stuff They Didn't Tell You

time since the Big Bang. Perhaps Einstein was right when he called his "cosmological constant" the biggest mistake he ever made.

If we logically accept the possibility that the pace of time throughout the cosmos has progressed and evolved (like everything else) over 13.8 billion years, then maybe we should be looking for something more logical that a fantastical force we cannot detect, or a cosmological constant Einstein rejected. The concept of the pace of time evolving in concert with the rest of the universe is much simpler and more esthetically beautiful. I chose to believe in simple and beautiful, even if it can't be tested with today's technology. Perhaps some day in the future we will know the truth…..

Newton & Einstein, Stuff They Didn't Tell You

TIME AND GRAVITY

Einstein observed that the force we feel from gravity is indistinguishable from the force we feel from acceleration (deceleration). In fact he defines gravity as acceleration caused by a large mass warping the fabric of space-time. Mass warps space-time by altering the pace of time (slowing time down) as we approach a large concentration of mass, such as a planet, star or black hole. We've all seen the famous video; a snooker ball rolls in a spiral around (apparently attracted to) a bowling ball that creates a depression (a gravity well) in the center of a rubber sheet.

Physicists, including Einstein, have spent decades trying to reconcile the mathematics of gravity (the world of the very large) with the theory of quantum mechanics (the world of the very very small). Perhaps that effort should be directed instead toward understanding the cosmic evolution of time, enabling us to someday directly manipulate the force of gravity to our own ends. This might be possible because the gravity well surrounding each mass in the universe is actually a "time well", i.e., a localized slowing of time.

We are all accustomed to defining velocity as the distance traveled by an object over a period of time (e.g., meters per second, where the number of meters traveled remains constant during each second of measurement). We are also accustomed to defining acceleration as a continuous increase (or decrease) in velocity per unit of time (e.g., meters per second squared, where the number of meters traveled changes during each new second of measurement). We have always assumed in these calculations that time is running at a constant (unchanging) pace for the duration of interest. We are not accustomed to defining acceleration as an unchanging velocity (including zero) that is measured while the pace of time is changing (i.e., each new second during that measurement is changing in duration). However, mathematically these two definitions should be identical.

Newton & Einstein, Stuff They Didn't Tell You

Calculus allows us to integrate a distance traveled over an interval of time (velocity). We can further integrate a change in velocity over an interval of time (acceleration). But how do we integrate a constant velocity (including zero) over a period of time where the pace of time is changing? We may need to invent a new type of calculus to do that? And that may require a new understanding of how time has evolved across the cosmos since the Big Bang.

If mass warps the space-time continuum by slowing the pace of time, the more concentrated matter becomes the slower time progresses. Indeed, if all matter in the universe were concentrated in one location (i.e., a singularity) time would logically stop completely, i.e., the pace of time would be zero. Actually, there would be no need for time because nothing would be changing. In the first few moments of the Big Bang the pace of time in the cosmos likely went from zero to some very slow pace compared to what we see today, because all matter was still concentrated in a relatively small space. As matter and space expanded the pace of time in the cosmos gradually increased, eventually reaching the value we observe today in our little corner of the universe.

If time we measure on Earth today is moving faster than it was five or ten billion years ago, then our estimate of the age of the universe may be off a bit. In fact it may be off a great deal. If we assume that the rate of time's progression has been a linear function from the moment of the Big Bang (time equals zero) to the present day then the universe is approximately half as old as previously thought, e.g., 7 billion years (as measured today) instead of 13.8 billion years. That also means that distances to distant stars and galaxies may be only half of our previous estimates. If time has accelerated since the Big Bang consistent with an exponential decrease in matter's rate of expansion then the apparent error in the age of the universe could be larger than one-half. To calculate the true age of the universe (as measured in today's time on earth) we would need to integrate the change in the pace of time over the apparent 13.8 billion years since the Big Bang. Integrating the change in the pace of time over that long a period may be beyond our reach at the moment. Still it is conceivable that the age of the universe and distances to other galaxies are much less than previously believed.

Newton & Einstein, Stuff They Didn't Tell You

If we could develop a means to manipulate the pace of time at any specific location we could manipulate the force of gravity. By creating localized changes in the pace of time we could direct the resultant forces toward whatever purpose we desire. We could create a local gravity well opposing that of the Earth's mass, using it to propel spacecraft to distant worlds, make heavy objects weightless for ease of transportation, or repel meteors that threaten our home planet. The technological opportunities presented by the ability to manipulate the pace of time are beyond current imagination.

Printed in Great Britain
by Amazon